KIDS EXPLORE AMERICA'S HISPANIC HERITAGE

2nd edition

Westridge Young Writers Workshop

John Muir Publications
Santa Fe, New Mexico

This book is dedicated to people of different cultures,
with the hope that they are proud of who they are.

John Muir Publications, P.O. Box 613, Santa Fe, NM 87504
Copyright © 1996, 1994 by Jefferson County School District No. R-1
Cover © 1994 by John Muir Publications

Printed in the United States of America
Second edition. First printing September 1996

Library of Congress Cataloging-in-Publication Data
Kids explore America's Hispanic heritage / Westridge Young Writers
    Workshop.— 2nd ed.
    p.   cm.
    Includes index.
    Summary: Presents writings by students in grades three to seven on
topics of Hispanic culture, including dance, cooking, games, history, art, songs,
and role models.
    ISBN 1-56261-272-7
    1. Hispanic Americans—Juvenile literature. 2. Children's writings, American.
    [1. Hispanic Americans. 2. Children's writings.]   I. Westridge Young Writers Workshop.
    E184.S75K53   1996
    973'.0468—dc20   91-42232
                                                                     CIP
                                                                      AC

Editors Rob Crisell, Peggy Schaefer, Elizabeth Wolf
Production Marie Vigil, Nikki Rooker
Design Susan Surprise
Printer Publishers Press

Distributed to the book trade by
Publishers Group West
Emeryville, California

Photo Credits   Photos on pages 13, 14, 15, 16, 19, 21, and 38 courtesy of
                 Denver Public Library Western History Department.
                 Photo on page 11 courtesy of Colorado Historical Society.

CONTENTS

ACKNOWLEDGMENTS / v

STUDENTS' PREFACE / vi

TEACHERS' PREFACE / vii

HISTORY / 1
The Meeting of Different Cultures / 1
Christopher Columbus / 2
Other Explorers / 4
New Money, New World / 9
The Move North / 9
Building the Missions / 10
Anglos Move to Mexico / 12
Modern Problems and Responses / 13
Fighting Back Against Injustice / 15
Other Origins of Hispanic Culture / 17
Hispanics Today / 17
Our Famous Relatives / 19

FUN, FOOD, AND FESTIVALS / 23
Festivals / 23
Las Posadas / 23
The Day of the Three Kings / 24
Easter Season / 25
Cinco de Mayo / 27
The Day of the Dead / 27
Customs and Traditions / 29
Quinceanera / 29
Baptism / 29
Wedding / 31
Food / 32
Tortillas / 32
Salsa para los Niños / 33
Guacamole / 34
Huevos Rancheros / 34
Chorizo con Huevos / 34
Chicken Enchiladas / 34
Arrachera al Carbon / 34

Atole de Fresa / 35
Chocolate Mexicano / 36
Fruit Punch / 36
Paletas / 36
Dances / 37

ART / 43
Artists / 44
Consuelo Gonzalez Amezcua / 44
Carmen Lomas Garza / 44
Eduardo Chavez / 45
Octavio Medellin / 45
Gregorio Marzan / 46
Some Traditional Hispanic
Art Forms / 48
Retablos / 48
Santos / 48
Folk Art / 48
Folk Art Projects / 49
Piñatas / 49
Molas / 52
Luminarias / 53

FUN WITH WORDS / 55
Dichos / 55
Chistes / 55
Adivinanzas / 58
Cognates / 59
Spanish Place-Names / 60
Los Colores / 60
Frases / 61

CUENTOS / 61
Our Lady of Guadalupe / 63
La Llorona / 65
El Grillo / 66
Los Ratoncitos / 69
El Principe y los Pájaros / 70
The Legand of El Santo Niño / 72

FAMOUS FIRSTS AND HEROES / 75
Father Junípero Serra / 76
Loreta Janeta Velazquez / 78
Juan Guiteras / 78
Diego Rivera / 78
Dennis Chavez / 79
Luis Alvarez / 80
Hector Garcia / 80
Henry B. Gonzalez / 80
Anthony Quinn / 81
Dan Sosa / 82
Julian Nava / 83
Patrick Flores / 83
Jaime Escalante / 84
Rita Moreno / 85
Roberto Clemente / 86
Katherine Ortega / 87
Lee Trevino / 87
Vikki Carr / 88
Martin Sheen / 88
Joan Baez / 89
Ritchie Valens / 90
Vilma Martinez / 90
Antonia Novello / 91
Jose Feliciano / 92
Linda Ronstadt / 93
Edward James Olmos / 93
Federico Pena / 94
Jim Plunkett / 95
Jimmy Smits / 96
Gloria Estefan / 96
Nancy Lopez / 97
Evelyn Cisneros / 97
Ellen Ochoa / 98
Fernando Valenzuela / 99
Tony Melendez / 99
Michael Carbajal / 102
Giselle Fernandez / 102
Selena / 102
More Famous Firsts and Heroes / 102

REAL PEOPLE—HISPANICS IN AMERICA TODAY / 106
Tino Mendez / 107
Bernadette Vigil / 108
Sidney Atencio / 109
Bennie and Lil Razo / 111
Pete Valdez / 112
Alicia Fernandez-Mott / 114
Sylvia Telles Ryan / 116
The Martinez Family / 117
Bishop Roberto Gonzales / 121
Homero E. Acevedo II / 122
Mary Ann A. Zapata / 124
Carlos Flores, M.D. / 125

YOUNG PEOPLE WHO MAKE A DIFFERENCE / 127
Ismael Hernandez / 128
Sarah Ramos / 129
Rick Alire / 130
Mary Rodas / 131
Brian Roybal / 132
Charlotte Lopez / 134

OUR VISION FOR A BETTER TOMORROW / 136

STUDENT AUTHORS / 137

TEACHER PARTICIPANTS / 138

CALENDAR / 139

RESOURCE GUIDE / 141

INDEX / 147

ACKNOWLEDGMENTS

We, the 110 student authors, are especially thankful to the people of Hispanic background who shared their time, talents, history, and knowledge with us while we were writing this book. We would also like to thank the Westridge Elementary School staff, the Westridge PTA, Ron Horn, Rose Roy, Josh Herald, Ruth Maria Acevedo, and all of our teachers for their confidence in us young writers.

Special thanks goes to several businesses and organizations for their financial support. Student scholarships were donated by King Soopers, Denver, Colorado, and Lakewood Civitan Club, Lakewood, Colorado. Teacher scholarships were donated by Adolph Coor's Company, Golden, Colorado. We want to thank Pam Faro, Storyteller, Lafayette, Colorado; Barbara Bustillos of Bustillos Productions, Arvada, Colorado; Our Lady of Guadalupe Dancers, Our Lady of Guadalupe Catholic Church, Denver, Colorado; Ron Rich, Publisher of *Booktalk*, Lakewood, Colorado; Father Tomás Fraile of St. Cajetan's Catholic Church, Denver, Colorado; and Candy's Tortilla, Denver, Colorado, for their donations of services and supplies.

Thanks also to the IBM Corporation for donating computers on which we did word processing.

STUDENTS' PREFACE

I'm proud to be me,
'Cause that's who I am.
Be proud to be you,
'Cause that's who you are.
The differences between us
Help us all to grow.
They strengthen our hearts,
So our pride can show.
Respect all others and they'll respect you.
Be kind to everyone in all that you do.
What's in this book you will need to know,
If you want to learn and you want to grow.
Explore different cultures—or maybe your own—
As we teach you of customs and stories well-known.

This book is fun, interesting, and cool—and it's from a kid's point of view. We authors are 110 students in grades three through seven. We think it was worth using part of our summer to write *Kids Explore America's Hispanic Heritage* instead of just watching TV or riding bikes. We're excited because this book will be available all over the United States, and it will help Americans enjoy a unique part of their heritage. This book is not just for kids, though. *Kids Explore America's Hispanic Heritage* is a great opportunity for everyone to learn. We've opened the door and given you just a special look into one culture.

TEACHERS' PREFACE

A dream is only a dream,
Until you take action
And make it a reality.
This dream was the hard work of many.

Many people may wonder how this book was started. It was conceived at Westridge Elementary School in Jefferson County, a western suburb of Denver, Colorado. Book publishing is a well-established part of the school curriculum. John Muir Publications of Santa Fe, New Mexico, was enthusiastic about our idea for a series of books—all written by children—on different cultures within the United States. Now there are six books in the "Kids Explore" series, including books on African American, Japanese American, Jewish, and Hispanic heritages, as well as a book on the gifts of kids with special needs.

We developed the plans for this volume in a summer enrichment class. During that class, students were exposed to the various aspects of Hispanic heritage that they would later write about. They discovered dances, cooking, games, history, art, songs, and real people in the Hispanic community. They researched, word processed, illustrated, organized, wrote, and proofread.

While students enhanced their writing skills and acquired firsthand knowledge of Hispanic culture, we teachers earned college credit through a course entitled "Integrating Hispanic Studies into the School Curriculum." Most of us are Hispanic, and our desire to learn more about our culture fueled our enthusiasm. We all explored ways to integrate Hispanic culture into the curriculum, improving our knowledge of publishing procedures and the process of writing. It was our goal to produce a book that would be a valuable addition to school libraries and programs.

The student writers, most of whom are Hispanic, are from the Denver area. They represent diverse economic and cultural backgrounds. Scholarship funds were available from the business community for those students who needed them.

Our students love being full-fledged authors and basking in the limelight that publication generates. All of us are very proud to be a part of this book.

HISTORY

Important people are sculpting our land.
Fighting, exploring, lending a hand.
Help us hold on to our past
As we reach into the future
And build it to last.

Welcome to Hispanic history. We'll look into some of the events and people of Hispanic culture from the 1400s to the present. Starting in the 1400s—the century when the Spanish explorers came to the New World—can give us a clearer picture of how the Hispanic traditions found their way to our country. History can be fun, especially when we realize how history, like America's Hispanic heritage, affects each of us today.

When historians—people who study the past—write history books, they use many sources of information and sometimes spend years doing research. They use old diaries written by people long ago. They look through books that describe the past. They go through old pictures and photographs. They talk to senior citizens who

made history. By doing this, they try to piece together what life was like in the past. We have tried to be good historians. Our book covers many important people and events. If you're interested in one or more of these, the library is a terrific place to find out more information. If this part of our book gets you more interested in the history that shaped America's Hispanic heritage, we are excited!

In this brief history, we hope you will see how these events and people have brought together the Spanish and native groups, blending them into the Hispanic heritage of our country. We will use the Aztecs to show an example of one native civilization. We will share how the Tainos of Cuba interacted with Columbus, so you can understand how complicated the Spanish takeover of land in the New World really was. Then we will look at other

Mesa Verde in Colorado, a site of the ancient Anasazi civilization

explorers from Spain and how the different cultures treated one another. We will talk about missionaries and how they related to the Indians. Next we will get into the period when the United States became a country and needed more land. We will see how this changed the lives of the Mexican people who lived in the United States and made Mexico look at the United States a little differently.

We will look at people who fought for Hispanic rights. Cuba and Puerto Rico—two countries important to the Hispanics in America—will be reviewed as part of American history, too. Lastly, we will see a lot of

Hispanic people who are making names for themselves in the United States today.

THE MEETING OF DIFFERENT CULTURES

The ancestors of Hispanic people came from many different cultures. These cultures, which had been developing for many hundreds of years, lived in different parts of the world, thousands of miles from each other.

One of the original cultures of today's Hispanic people is the native people of the

Americas. We know these native people as Indians. Some of the Natives that influenced Hispanic culture lived in what is now Mexico, Cuba, Central America, the West Indies, and the United States. For thousands of years, these people lived in groups with their own traditions, values, and religious beliefs. In fact, many Indian cultures began in prehistoric times. Later on, other Indian cultures, such as the Aztecs of Mexico, the Incas of South America, the Mayas of Central America, the Arawaks of Puerto Rico, and the Tainos of Cuba, developed in this area. History shows that these Indians excelled in agriculture and hunting, but they also did great things in astronomy, mathematics, and architecture.

The Aztecs were an advanced culture for their time, which lasted from around A.D. 1100 to the 1520s. "Anno Domini" (A.D.) means "in the year of the Lord." The Aztecs built tall pyramids. They mined gold, silver, jade, and turquoise. Their capital city was Tenochtitlán [ten-och-teat-LON]. It was built

on land that was once a lake. The Aztecs drained the lake and filled it back up with dirt. Ever since this time, this area has had a great number of earthquakes because the ground is unstable. Mexico City is built right on top of the old city of Tenochtitlán.

Warning—this paragraph is for strong stomachs only! The Aztecs believed that to keep the sun moving across the sky, they needed to offer up to it something from a human body that moved all the time. So the Aztecs offered a human heart, which was taken quickly from sacrificial victims during one of their religious ceremonies. The Aztecs believed that human sacrifices could take away the sins of the people.

The Aztecs also had some cool names for their gods. Did you know that Quetzalcoatl [ket-sul-ko-AH-tul] created humankind? At

least, that's what the Aztecs thought. They built temples in his honor. Quetzalcoatl was shown in drawings with a serpent head and a bird body. The word "Quetzalcoatl" means "plumed serpent." The Aztecs also knew him as the god of wisdom. He told the ancestors of the Aztec people to stop sacrificing humans and start sacrificing animals. The people didn't like that and told him to leave. He said he would return from the East on a ship. Guess where the Spanish come into the picture?

There had been many different explorers in the region. Explorers are people who take risks by going somewhere they don't know much about. Can you imagine convincing the President of the United States to let you take a spaceship to travel to another planet? This is what it may have been like for early explorers.

Some people don't like to call the Spanish "explorers" because Indians were already living here. Indians probably thought of the Spanish as invaders, and we can see their point. We will refer to the Spanish as explorers, even though they really did act more like invaders most of the time. Because these explorers were mostly from Spain, many areas in the Western Hemisphere still speak Spanish today.

CHRISTOPHER COLUMBUS

In the 1400s, explorers from Spain crossed the ocean and discovered there were civilizations of people living in the part of the world we call Mesoamerica, which includes southern Mexico, Central America, and the West Indies. Christopher Columbus—whose Spanish name was Cristóbal Colón—was one of these explorers. He thought that by crossing the Atlantic Ocean, he would find an easier way to get to India. You see, if the Spanish wanted to trade with India, they had to pay a fee to every country on their way. This got very expensive. Columbus wanted to find an easier, cheaper way to travel around the world using the oceans. Many people thought that the world was flat. They thought Columbus would fall off the Earth when he got to the edge. This must not have bothered him much, because he was excited to make the voyage no matter what.

Columbus had been a mapmaker for the country of Portugal. He got his supplies for sailing from King Ferdinand and Queen

LEGEND

COLUMBUS	⫯⫯⫯	S = SPAIN
CORTEZ	∿∿	NA = NORTH AMERICAN
PIZARRO	•—•—•	SA = SOUTH AMERICA
P. DE LEON	◄◄◄	PUERTO RICO AND CUBA
		(ISLANDS)

Isabella of Spain. When Columbus set off on his voyage, others didn't know if he would make it. This is where the rhyme comes in: "In fourteen hundred and ninety-two, Columbus sailed the ocean blue." Instead of reaching his destination—India—Columbus found the New World. Historians say Columbus thought he was in India, so he called the people he met "Indians."

The king and queen of Spain were surprised and excited about Columbus' claims. They hoped Columbus might find gold or other valuables they could ship back to Spain, so they sent him again.

OTHER EXPLORERS

Juan Ponce de Leon went on Columbus' second trip to the New World in 1493. He and his crew landed on the shores of an island, and because of the riches they hoped to find there, they called it Puerto Rico (which means "Rich Port"). Here, the Spanish met the Taino Indians who lived in parts of Puerto Rico and Cuba with their relatives, the Arawaks.

There were many differences between the Spanish and the natives. First of all, the Spanish acted as though they owned everything. That's why they made claim to every territory they found. The native groups believed the land couldn't belong to anyone—that it was just part of nature. This is why the Indians didn't understand when the Spaniards claimed the land.

Another difference was how the two cultures felt about gold. For example, the Tainos told Ponce de Leon about the rivers of gold, because whenever he heard the word "gold," he would get excited. They told him there was lots of gold all over the place, even though it wasn't true. The Tainos didn't understand how important gold was to Ponce de Leon. It was not very special to the Tainos, so they didn't understand why he became so mean when he couldn't find it.

Ponce de Leon made the natives mine for the gold. This created problems between the Spanish and the natives. Taino weapons were useless against the more modern equipment of Spaniards. As in Cuba, many Tainos were killed in battle, and a lot also died from the diseases the Spanish brought with them. Measles, tuberculosis, and smallpox didn't exist in the New World until the Europeans brought them. If the natives didn't die from the diseases or in battles, they died from working in the mines. In fact, in Cuba and Puerto Rico together, more than 8 million Taino Indians died. So many Indians died that soon there weren't enough workers for the mines. Eventually, the Spanish brought slaves from Africa to work.

The diaries and writings of others such as Father Bartolome de las Casas show that many cruel things happened to the groups of native people Columbus and his men met. The last six years of the 1400s are known as the Black Legend in Spanish history. Columbus and his brothers were governors in Cuba. They ruled and were cruel to the Tainos. Some Indians were tortured for not following the Spanish laws,

many of which they didn't understand. They sometimes had their hands cut off as a penalty.

Many things like this also happened when other Spanish and European explorers settled the New World. More details about Columbus can be found in his ship's log, which has been translated into English, and in the diaries and reports of other explorers and missionaries.

In 1509, Ponce de Leon became governor of Puerto Rico, making it a Spanish colony. Ponce de Leon left his mark on Puerto Rico. Today one of the largest cities in Puerto Rico is named Ponce.

Americans remember Ponce de Leon because he explored and named Florida ("Place of Flowers"). He was looking for a legendary fountain. The legend said if you drank or bathed from this special fountain, you would stay young forever. This fountain was called the Fountain of Youth. Do you think Ponce de Leon found this fountain before he disappeared in 1513?

In 1519, another Spanish explorer named Hernán Cortés came looking for gold. When he arrived in Mexico, the Aztecs remembered the legend of Quetzalcoatl, the man who had the serpent's head and a bird's body. Quetzalcoatl left the Aztecs and said that when he came back on his ship, he would have light skin and a beard. So when Cortés arrived, the Aztecs thought he and his men were gods. They gave him gold and jewels and lots of respect. When one of Cortés' men was injured and blood came out of his injury, the Aztecs began to wonder if Cortés was really a god.

Like the explorers before him, Cortés soon became cruel to the Aztecs. He took advantage of the Aztecs' kindness and started to demand gold and treasure—more gold than even a god would need. He punished the Aztecs if they didn't move or work to dig for gold as fast as he told them to. Sometimes he would snip off the tips of their noses or ears if they disobeyed him. The Aztec leader sent a message for Cortés to leave, but Cortés didn't want to.

Many groups who were enemies of the Aztecs joined Cortés in a great battle against them. The Aztecs had clubs, spears, and axes. The Spanish had weapons that were advanced for their time, so Cortés and the Spanish beat the Aztecs and captured the city of Tenochtitlán in 1521.

Alvarar Nuñez Cabeza de Vaca was another Spanish conqueror who was on an expedition to capture Indians to make them slaves for the Spanish. He was shipwrecked in the Gulf of Mexico in 1528 and accidentally became an explorer when he was trying to save his life. He walked from Indian group to Indian group trying to get home. Cabeza de Vaca would have died if the Indians hadn't helped him. He heard stories from the Indians about golden riches north of Mexico. (Remember that the Indians didn't think about gold the same way the Spaniards did.) Cabeza de Vaca was very sick, so he didn't go after the gold. When he got better, he went back to Mexico and told the Spanish leaders about the gold. Cabeza de Vaca should have known that the people who had helped him would be made into slaves to find the gold. When the Spaniards went looking for the gold, this is exactly what happened. Cabeza de Vaca ended up hurting the people who had been kind to him and had helped him stay alive. He was sad for a long time because of what had happened to the Indians who had helped him.

"Gold! Gold! I want to find the Seven Cities of Gold!" cried Francisco de Coronado, another Spanish explorer. Coronado was the first European to travel around what we now call the southwestern United States. He brought horses to the natives so that the slaves could do more work in the fields. He also accidentally brought smallpox, which wiped out many of the Indians. He had heard about seven cities in the northern part of Mexico—now the United States—that were made out of gold. He was disappointed when he found the small Indian villages in the areas that are now Arizona, New Mexico, Colorado, and Kansas. He never found any cities made of gold. When he came back to Mexico, nobody thought he was a real explorer because he never found what he had gone looking for.

NEW MONEY, NEW WORLD

With all the silver and gold the native people were mining for the Spaniards, the time was right to make coins. Some of the first mints—places where coins are made by the government—were built by the Spanish. In the 1500s and 1600s, the coins were made by beating out a thin stamp of silver or gold into a shape that contained the Spanish royal coat of arms. These

rough coins are known as Cobbs and can still be found on the ocean floor from Spanish ships that sunk off the coast of Florida, the Caribbean, and all over the Gulf of Mexico. Often, ships were overloaded with treasure, trying to take as much as possible back to Spain.

The coin presses multiplied, and Spain minted its famous eight *reales* [ray-ALL-ace] starting in the early 1700s. Spain had mints in its homeland, in Mexico, and all over South America. It put different marks on the coins telling where they were made. When people couldn't get the right change to buy or sell something, they just chopped these coins up like a pizza into smaller pieces. This is where the terms "bits" and "pieces of eight" come from.

Many of these eight reales, also called pillar dollars, were used as money all over the United States because early American currency was often hard to get. Early colonists in the northern United States used this currency.

THE MOVE NORTH

For many reasons, the people of the Middle Americas were urged to move to the north. Besides Mexico, the Spanish claimed a giant territory that included the present-day states of California, Nevada, Utah, Colorado, New Mexico, Arizona, and Texas. In 1821, Mexico declared its freedom from Spain, so the Mexican flag flew over this area. However, the Mexicans began to lose their land in the 1840s. In less than 50 years, the land that is now the southwestern part of the United States had changed hands three times. This all began when the Spanish moved north.

Some Spaniards wanted more land, some wanted gold, and some wanted to spread Christianity. The Spanish also moved north because there was not much food in the south. However, there were already people living in the area in the north.

The people moving to the north had to develop a plan. They decided to build villages. They used adobe bricks to make houses called *haciendas* [ah-see-EN-dahs]. A fort was built in each village where soldiers could stay to watch over the church and the Spaniards. The Spanish forced natives to build missions. In return, the Spanish promised to use the mission to protect the Indians from other native groups that weren't friendly with them. Most Indians did not own land or territory or have any interest in gold until the Europeans made it necessary to do so. A few warlike tribes fought over natural resources, but they were the exceptions. Most Indians greeted the Spaniards peacefully.

BUILDING THE MISSIONS

One of the goals of missions was to convert the native people to Christianity. The missionaries did this in many ways. The Spaniards brought the Indians to the mission, usually by force. Once the Indians were there, they were not allowed to leave. The Indians were baptized and converted to the Catholic religion. In the missions, the Indians had to do the farming, building, weaving, and blacksmithing. If they tried to escape, the Spanish soldiers treated them cruelly. They might even cut off a foot or a hand or smash an ankle to keep them from running away. Not all missions were this bad, though.

The way the Indians had lived before the Spanish came was very different from the way they lived in the missions. There was less space, more people, and the food they were forced to eat was strange to them. Their rooms were tiny and not very clean. It was a bad situation. The new diseases brought to them made the Indians weak, and they got sick a lot. More than half the native people in the missions died from

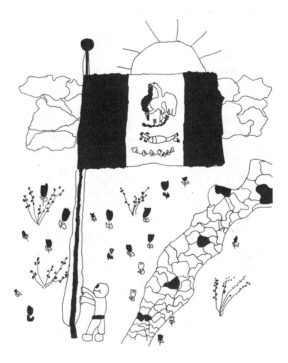

Depiction of the Spanish discovery of the Mississippi River in May 1541

smallpox or bubonic plague. Think about it this way: If you had four people in your family, two or three might die.

Still, the missions were very important in settling the land the explorers claimed, even though some people aren't sure if the missionaries really helped the people who had lived there before them.

The first colony in what is now the southwestern United States was built by Juan de Oñate. The king of Spain gave Oñate permission to take some people from Mexico with him to the land now known as New Mexico. The people he took included Spanish soldiers, natives, missionaries, and mestizos. (Mestizos are people who have one parent who is Spanish and one parent who is Indian.) By 1630, there were 25 missions throughout New Mexico. Oñate became the governor of Santa Fe. He called his place of government *El Palacio de los Gobernadores*, the Palace of the Governors.

Father Junípero Serra was a missionary in California. In the 1700s, he helped people build missions to live in. San Francisco, Los Angeles, and San Diego were among 21 missions established along a route called El Camino Real—"the Royal Road"—

a road connecting all of the missions. Today, this road is named U.S. 101, a major highway along the California coast.

Aianasio Dominguez and Silvestre Velez de Escalante were two missionaries who traveled together in 1776. They left from what we now call Santa Fe, New Mexico, to travel through Colorado, Utah, Arizona, and New Mexico to find new paths to California. They never made it to California. They thought teaching Christianity to the Indians they met along the way was more important. They also kept a diary of what they saw each day. Judging from reading their diary, their trip sounded very challenging.

Dominguez and Escalante's expedition ran into many problems. Sometimes the weather wasn't good. Sometimes the trails were rough. One time they shared some food with the Sabuagana Yutas Indians. One Indian ate so much that he got sick. He started to blame Dominguez and Escalante

and their men, who were afraid that they would be in danger if the Indians found out about the stomach problem. But the Indian who had eaten too much finally threw up. Then he felt better and everything was fine again.

A priest named Miguel Hidalgo lived in the 1800s. He wanted to help the Indians in Mexico, so he taught them to grow their own crops and to do things for themselves. He and the Indians went to Mexico City to seek protection against the Spanish soldiers. But Father Hidalgo was captured and killed. Today, the Mexicans call him the Father of Mexico.

ANGLOS MOVE TO MEXICO

When the Anglos (white people who are not Hispanic) came into the Mexican territories, they did pretty well. Many of them learned the language, converted to the Catholic religion, and got along with the people who lived there. When more Anglos came, though, Mexico started to lose control of its territories. The ways of the American merchants and trappers didn't mix with the ways of the Mexicans. The customs and traditions of the different people in this area were confusing to everyone. The native Mexicans were concerned with the trapping and hunting that the American merchants and trappers did. Americans who came into the area were often aggressive. The Mexicans were often more humble and more formal.

The Alamo was built in 1836. This is how it looks today in San Antonio, Texas.

Because of these differences, fighting began in 1835. The Anglos believed the territory they called Texas belonged to them. The Anglos started taking over small military places from the Mexicans. Then in December of 1835, the Anglos took the Alamo, a mission that had been made into a military building in San Antonio. The president of Mexico said this action was unfair. He sent troops across the Rio Grande to get the land back for Mexico because he felt the Anglos had no business being there. The Mexicans attacked the Alamo and took control. While they were resting after the battle, another Texan army surprised them, shouting "Remember the Alamo!" More than 600 Mexican soldiers were killed in the Battle of San Jacinto on April 21, 1836. After this, Texas became an independent republic. This was the start of Mexico's loss of its northern land holdings.

MODERN PROBLEMS AND RESPONSES

Problems about land had been building up for years because the United States wanted to move its boundaries all the way to the Pacific Ocean. The United States had tried to make a deal to buy one part of northern Mexico, but Mexico didn't want to sell it. This started the Mexican-American War.

There was no way the president of Mexico and his people could protect the Mexican territory they had lived in all their lives. In a year, Mexico had lost the lands that are now the states of California, Nevada, Utah, New Mexico, Colorado, Wyoming, and parts of Arizona. The United States was larger than Mexico after gaining this land. The Treaty of Guadalupe Hidalgo in 1848 ended the Mexican-American War. By the terms of the treaty, the United States gained one-third of Mexico. The Hispanics who lived in the area that used to be Mexico were suddenly living in the United States. Many of the Anglo Americans didn't respect these new Mexican residents. The Americans disobeyed the promises of the treaty. They didn't give the Hispanics full citizenship or property rights, and they wouldn't even let them speak their own language. The Americans discouraged the Hispanics from having their own religion, culture, and customs.

Many of the American laws did not seem fair to the Hispanics and other non-Anglos. Americans treated the new residents unfairly by telling the Hispanics the American laws in English. The Hispanics did not understand this language, so they were often cheated out of their land. The Hispanic people were so confused about what was going on that the Anglos took advantage of them.

One of the laws that was unfair to Hispanics and to black Americans said that is was illegal for them to be on a jury. This law

A Spanish mission in the 1700s, probably in Mexico

lasted until 1954. Some states made it illegal to speak Spanish in schools. Before the Bilingual Education Act in 1968, children couldn't be taught in any language but English. So if they only spoke Spanish, too bad! Until 1970, a law in California said that you had to be able to read the Constitution in English before you could vote. People even had to take an English test before they could vote.

Another example of prejudice occurred in 1946. Zoot suits were then popular among young Mexican American men. Zoot-suit pants had a high waistline and were tapered at the ankles. The long suit jackets came down to the knees. Zoot suits were common in California as well as other parts of the United States. But being part of a group was not always good for Mexican American men. Once, sailors on leave in California attacked Mexican Americans in zoot suits. Police did nothing to stop the sailors from beating up the young zoot-suiters. The newspapers reported that the zoot-suiters had started violent riots and they were arrested. The government wouldn't listen to the growing Hispanic problems. This made the Hispanics feel helpless and angry.

FIGHTING BACK AGAINST INJUSTICE

Hispanic workers had generally not been treated well on the job. One of the most difficult jobs was to work as a migrant worker. Migrant workers are people who move

Migrant farm worker

from area to area, crop to crop, picking fruit and vegetables for small wages. The Spanish word for them is *brazeros* [brah-SAY-ros], which means "people who work with their arms." These migrant workers often had to travel because they needed to search for a new job when they finished harvesting the fruit, vegetables, or crops in one area. Not only was the work hard, but the houses were overcrowded and not good. There were no doctors for them if they got sick. Migrant workers tried to organize as early as 1883. *Vaqueros* [vah-KEH-rohs]— Mexican American cowboys—organized a strike for better pay in Texas that same year. Between 1900 and 1930, Mexican Americans led or took part in miners' strikes.

Cesar Chavez and his family were migrant

Protest in Denver

workers. He knew Hispanics needed to get organized. They needed leadership. For example, when the Mexican American migrant workers tried to earn money and get a better life in the United States, business owners were often unfair to them. They had the migrant workers do the work, then paid them very little money. Hispanics knew something had to be done to help improve the living conditions of their people. They needed to get together and decide what to do about their problems in the United States.

Cesar Chavez didn't like the way migrant workers were treated. He started the National Farm Workers Association in 1962. This was a union to get better pay. Did you know that Mr. Chavez once didn't eat for 36 days? He didn't eat because he was protesting the poor living conditions the brazeros lived in. He wanted to show people he was serious, so he went on a hunger strike. He also redefined the meaning of the word "Chicano" so that people would understand it better. Chicano used to be one of the worst words a person

could use to refer to a Mexican person.

The parents of many Hispanic children wanted to fit into Anglo American society and forget their past heritage. Inspired by Mr. Chavez, their children joined together by calling themselves "Chicanos." Instead of trying to mix into the Anglo way of life, these children adopted an identity they felt proud of. In 1993, Cesar Chavez died at the age of 56. He worked hard to help his people and tried to make the world a better place.

There have been other Hispanic workers who tried to join unions for better treatment and better pay, but some unions didn't accept them. So the Hispanics formed their own union called the *Confederación de Uniones Obreras Mexicanos* (Confederation of Unions of Mexican Workers, CUOM). By doing this, they were protesting against the people

Cesar Chavez

who were unfair to them. In 1929, a group of Hispanics formed a group called the League of United Latin American Citizens (LULAC). They wanted to help Hispanic people be good, patriotic citizens, learn English, get more education, and be treated equally. LULAC still exists today.

OTHER ORIGINS OF HISPANIC CULTURE

Do you know all the places that you will find the Hispanic culture? Read on. Cuba is a big island—almost 746 miles long. That's almost the same as the distance from New York to Chicago. Cuba was a Spanish colony for a long time because of the Spanish explorers who landed there. That's why a lot of Cuban culture and customs are Hispanic.

In the early 1960s, many Cubans came to the United States because their country's government became Communist and they didn't think they could live there anymore. Many went to Miami, Florida, just 90 miles away. Imagine having to choose between staying with your family and friends or leaving your country for a new one. One person who did this is Tino Mendez, who was 17 years old when he left Cuba for freedom in the United States. Look for his story in the "Real People" section of this book.

Puerto Rico is a small island off the coast of Florida. The island itself is only 100 miles by 35 miles and about the size of Connecticut. Puerto Ricans have been citizens of the United States since 1917. Puerto Rico is a commonwealth of the United States. That means it's almost like a state. Puerto Rico never did live up to its name of being a "rich port." Many people had to move to the mainland in the 1960s because of problems with hunger and finding jobs. The first to come to the mainland of the United States were garment workers—people who make clothes for a living. They mostly went to New York because they got the best jobs there. More than 2 million Puerto Ricans live in this country, and half of them live in New York. New York's Puerto Rican population is second only to that of Puerto Rico's capital, San Juan. Read about Bishop Roberto Gonzales and Dr. Carlos Flores, two Puerto Rican-Americans, in the "Real People" section of our book.

HISPANICS TODAY

Other Hispanic organizations are working to improve their communities, too. The United States Hispanic Chamber of Commerce is a business organization that helps Latino people set up and be successful at running their businesses. These businesses help improve the economic level of the communities where they're located by providing job opportunities.

Other Hispanic groups are working to improve education and recognize good role models for young people. Many communities have started programs like "The Hispanic Salute," which gives scholarships to outstanding Hispanic youth and recognizes adult leaders.

The Mexican American Legal Defense and Education Fund (MALDEF) works for the protection of civil rights and equal opportunities for Hispanics in education and employment. MALDEF filed a discrimination suit against the National Park Service, which resulted in a new hiring and promotion policy for Hispanics in park service. With the help of organizations like MALDEF, Hispanics and African Americans filed a lawsuit against the Los Angeles Schools. This suit accused the L.A. School District of placing experienced, higher-paid teachers in white neighborhoods and of not allowing minority kids equal educational resources. Because of the lawsuit, the L.A. School District has agreed to start addressing these problems in 1997. Groups like LULAC and MALDEF are continuing the fight to improve schools.

Hispanics are working to solve other big problems. They want to improve their image in the media because they are often shown in negative ways or not at all. Television hasn't been much better. To fight these harmful portrayals, Hispanics in many cities have started special media programs of their own to share news that Latinos need. Many cities have newspapers for Hispanic communities, including Los Angeles, New York City, Denver, Miami, and Chicago. You can also read about these Hispanics in magazines such as *Hispanic*, *Temas*, and *Replica*. *La Familia de Hoy* ("The Family of Today") was a magazine that began in 1990 and has already has sold more than 165,000 issues.

The number of Hispanic television and radio stations across the nation is also growing. Because of the large number of Hispanics and their hard work in this country, the Spanish language media will continue to help the Hispanic culture and provide employment opportunities.

People have argued about affirmative action programs for many years. In fact, this issue is still debated in the 1990s. Affirmative action programs were started in the 1960s to help overcome prejudice against minorities. It encouraged employers to hire a certain percentage of minorities in their companies, so that everyone would have equal opportunities to compete for jobs. Some people feel affirmative action has really helped some minorities get better jobs. Others feel affirmative action is unfair because they believe minorities are being given jobs even if they aren't as qualified as others. They think this is reverse discrimination. Recently, the university system in California changed its affirmative action policies and won't have special rules for minorities to get into their schools. Many Hispanic leaders are studying affirmative action to help people understand it better.

In another issue, Hispanics are concerned about the immigration debate in this country. In 1990, President Bush signed an immigration act that increased legal immigration by 40 percent. Two years later, Attorney General William Barr announced a plan to increase the guards for the U.S.-Mexican border. In 1993, President Clinton spoke for a crackdown on people who

Statue honoring Private José Martinez, Denver, Colorado

smuggle illegal aliens into the U.S. He also asked for more money from Congress to strengthen border controls.

Some non-Hispanics worry that the legal Hispanic population will not become a part of the English-speaking culture. Others are concerned that the Spanish-speaking minority will be unable to find good jobs because of language and education problems.

Hispanics today are working to solve problems on issues like illegal immigration, "English Only" laws, lack of funding for public education, and the end to gains made under affirmative action programs. They know there aren't easy answers to these problems. Finding a solution will take hard work and perseverance.

Thanks partly to Hispanic culture, the United States is becoming more multilingual, multicultural, and more diverse than ever before in its history. If you look at a map from the last census, you can see that America's Hispanic population is growing. It is predicted that by the year 2000, Hispanics will be the largest minority in the country. We know that all Americans need to work together for our country's future, so that our citizens can share the richness of their many heritages. If we work hard, we can accomplish this goal.

OUR FAMOUS RELATIVES

Out of the 110 authors who participated in our writing workshop, at least three of us have famous relatives. One was Diego Archuleta, born in 1813. Another was Casmiro Barela, who was born in 1847. The last relative in our "Hall of Fame" is Rudolfo "Corky" Gonzales, who is still living today. We hope you enjoy reading about our relatives and finding out why they are famous.

Diego Archuleta
by Michael Laydon

It just so happens that my great-great-great-great-grandfather, Diego Archuleta, was involved in the fight over the Texas territory and the Alamo. Diego Archuleta was 22 years old when the Mexicans won the battle of the Alamo in 1835. Later, Diego was assigned a group of soldiers and was given the rank of lieutenant colonel of the militia by the Mexican government.

In 1841, when Mexico was invaded by the Texas–Santa Fe Expedition, Archuleta was in command of the troops that assisted in the capture of the Texans. In 1843, he was elected deputy of the National Mexican Congress of New Mexico. He received the Golden Cross Award for guarding the Mexican territory.

Archuleta was appointed second in command of the Mexican military. A few years later, he wanted to fight, but he knew it was an impossibility because of the increasing numbers of Anglos moving to the area.

Diego Archuleta

Casimiro Barela

When my great-great-great-great-grandfather died, his funeral was the biggest ever in Santa Fe, New Mexico. Anyone would be proud to have someone like him in the family tree!

Casimiro Barela
by James Barela

My great-great-great-uncle, Casimiro Barela, has been featured in a couple of biography books written by kids. He was born in 1847, in Embudo, New Mexico. His father, José, had pushed him to work hard so he would be successful in life. It looks like this advice paid off because Barela became a very famous person.

Barela helped write the Constitution of Colorado. He helped make laws that benefited and protected Hispanics. He also served for 40 years as a state senator of Colorado. Casimiro Barela spent more than

half of his life as a senator! He even had a town in southern Colorado named after him—Barela. There is a stained glass window of Senator Barela in the Colorado State Capitol. If you're ever in Denver, check it out. Casimiro Barela is a great man to have as a great-great-great-uncle.

Rudolfo ("Corky") Gonzalez
by Sergio Gonzalez

Another person who was a leader in the Hispanic movement was Rudolfo Gonzalez. He wrote a book called *I Am Joaquin* (*Yo Soy Joaquin*) and started a group called "Crusade for Justice" to improve the pride of Hispanics. He was a leader in the Chicano movement. Because he is my grandfather, he will be called "Gramps" in the rest of this article.

Gramps came to our writing class for this book and spoke about many things. He told

Rudolfo "Corky" Gonzalez

us that it is important to know where we come from so we can know who we are. It is important to learn our culture. We can learn about our culture from our family, on our own, or from books. But we have to know who our ancestors were, or else we can't know who we are and what our culture is.

"We can all be different, but we have the same father, God," Gramps said. "We are all one, and we can still be friends, because we are all on the same Earth. Just taking over a whole group of people is wrong, because people aren't like play toys. They are real."

Gramps also told us that reading books is an important way for us to learn. They can tell us about our culture or about anything we want to know. To get books, Gramps worked for "Uncle Bob," who was not a relative, just a special person. In "Uncle Bob's" pawn shop, there was a big shelf of books about Hispanics and other groups. Gramps couldn't find these kinds of books in other places. He learned a lot from books and believes that they are important and should be treasured.

Gramps told all of the young authors that we were making his dream come true by writing a book about Hispanics.

This is the end of a very brief look at the Hispanic history of America. To get a more complete picture, you need to read several books and talk to lots of different people. It is hard work, but we think you will have a good time doing it.

FUN, FOOD, AND FESTIVALS

There are fiestas here.
There are recipes, too.
Fun, food, and festivals,
They are all for you.

FESTIVALS

Festivals are a special time for bringing Hispanic families together. This part of our book touches on some religious and nonreligious celebrations. These Hispanic celebrations are full of laughter and joy. Many Hispanics have adopted American customs. Some Hispanic families now include the Christmas tree and Santa Claus as part of their Christmas traditions as well as *Las Posadas* and *luminarias*. Think about Hispanic customs you see in America as you read about Las Posadas, the Day of the Three Kings, Easter, Cinco de Mayo, Quinceanera, and Day of the Dead.

Las Posadas

If you take part in Las Posadas, you probably will remember it until the end of time.

In most Spanish-speaking countries of the Americas, this special Christmas tradition begins on December 16. It is a Christmas play of Spanish heritage that was first performed hundreds of years ago in Europe.

This event brings to life how Joseph and Mary searched for a place for the Christ Child to be born. The word *posada* means "inn" or "place of lodging." If you remember the story, Joseph and Mary could not find an inn where Mary could give birth, so they wandered until they found a stable with a manger.

To celebrate Las Posadas in the traditional way, people go from house to house and knock on the doors of friends and neighbors every night for nine days. They pretend to be searching for a place for Jesus to be born. They carry lanterns and small figures of Mary and Joseph. They create what is called a Nativity scene. They sing or recite poems wherever they go. It's similar to going caroling.

When they reach the house in which the Nativity scene will be kept for the night, they have a big celebration. One of the foods people have is tamales. They're made of pork or beef in a red chili-sauce dough, wrapped in a corn husk, and then steamed.

Las Posadas is celebrated by many Hispanic people, though the details may be different. For example, in Mexico, a posada party would have a piñata [peen-YAH-tah]. A piñata is a clay pot or frame covered with frilly paper and filled with candy or trinkets. You can find out how to make a piñata in the Art chapter of this book. Try it out for yourself.

Many parts of Christmas in America have taken on Hispanic customs. All across our nation you can hear people say, *"Feliz Navidad"* [fay-LEES nah-vee-DAHD], which is Spanish for "Merry Christmas." It is not

unusual for different kinds of churches and communities to celebrate Las Posadas by having real people dress up as Mary and Joseph and ride on a live donkey. Luminarias—containers or bags filled with lighted candles—are often used to decorate for Las Posadas or Christmas activities. In fact, Phoenix, Arizona, lights its Desert Botanical Garden with 6,000 luminarias for Christmas celebrations. Albuquerque, New Mexico, and San Antonio, Texas, are only two of many American communities that schedule an annual Las Posadas celebration.

The Day of the Three Kings

Some people might think it's strange to have Christmas in January. On January 6,

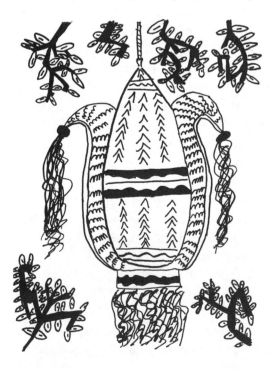

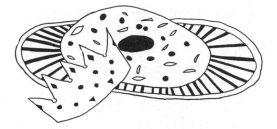

the Day of the Three Kings is celebrated. This special holiday comes exactly 12 days after the infant Jesus was born. This tradition comes from the Bible. According to the Bible, the Three Kings traveled 12 days to bring their gifts to baby Jesus.

On the night of January 5, children leave their shoes or an empty shoe box stuffed with straw outside their house for the camels that the Three Kings ride. In the morning, the straw is gone, and in its place, they find candy, fruit, and toys. This tradition reminds the children of the Three Kings' journey to find Jesus.

Some families might bake a festive kind of Hispanic bread to eat on this day. It is called Marzan bread. This holiday bread is shaped like a crown and has cherries and pineapple on it to represent jewels. It reminds the people of the crowns worn by the Three Kings. The baker puts a special surprise in the bread. It might be a small china doll, a charm, a coin, or even a ring. It is said that this object will bring good luck to the person who finds it.

In some places in Europe, the Day of the Three Kings is called "Little Christmas." Maybe it got that name because people received little presents. Many different churches celebrate the Day of the Three Kings in America. They call it Epiphany. A popular American Christmas song, "The Twelve Days of Christmas," might be related to this special day.

Easter Season

Easter is a religious holiday celebrated not only by Hispanics, but by Christians all over the world. Easter is the last day of a special season called Lent, which lasts for 40 days and nights before Easter Sunday. The last week of Lent is called "Holy Week." Many churches celebrate at least three special days. Holy Thursday is first.

This is when Jesus ate dinner with his apostles for the last time. The dinner is referred to as the "Last Supper." After Holy Thursday is Good Friday—the day before Jesus was nailed to the cross. On Sunday Easter is celebrated. The reason Christians

back and forth and sneak up behind a good friend and break the cascarone over his or her head.

Here are the directions for making cascarones:

1. Make a hole about the size of a dime in one end to drain the raw insides. You can either drink the egg in eggnog or fry it, but don't waste it.

2. Now clean the eggshell out by washing it. Let it dry. Start saving eggshells about three months before Easter.

3. When Easter is close, make confetti out of brightly colored paper and fill half of the eggshell with it.

4. Now make a paste with flour and water to cover up the hole.

celebrate this holiday is to honor the day Jesus rose from the dead. This holiday is in the spring when new life is beginning all around.

On Easter Sunday, many people wake up and go to church. After church, children go home to hunt for Easter eggs. Easter eggs are brightly decorated eggs that are hard-boiled or plastic eggs with candy inside. Often during this day, family members gather together for a big dinner.

Traditionally, Hispanics celebrate holidays with huge gatherings. Some Hispanics have special Easter eggs that are called *cascarones* [kahs-kah-RO-nays]. These eggs might be fun for your family to make. They are whole eggshells filled with colored confetti. Children like to act as if they are in battles when they throw the eggs

Cinco de Mayo

Cinco de Mayo (Fifth of May) is an exciting festival. This celebration takes place in many American cities across our nation as well as in Mexico. This has become a day for Mexican Americans to share their traditions with many friends of different heritages.

The history behind this day goes back to 1862, when Napoleon III was the leader of France. Mexico owed large sums of money to France. Napoleon used this as an excuse to have his soldiers invade Mexico. There was a fierce battle called the Battle of Puebla. The French army had many weapons and had been well trained before the battle. Puebla was a small farming town south of Mexico City. The vil-

lagers had to make their own army with very few guns and bullets. The Mexicans were ragged and poor, but they fought on until the French retreated. We were impressed by the courage of these Mexicans. This battle showed us that if you don't give up, you can win even if the odds are against you.

If you went to a Cinco de Mayo celebration in America, you might hear a mariachi band playing lively music and see beautiful dancers spinning in the streets. Vendors would be selling colorful Mexican crafts. You might hear someone calling, "Tacos, burritos, and enchiladas!" You would smell delicious scents in the air and feel the excitement everywhere. In the month of May, try to locate a Cinco de Mayo celebration in your community so you can celebrate, too!

The Day of the Dead

So many Hispanic customs have their beginnings in completely different cultures. This holiday is a good example. Many native groups that lived in the New World had customs that showed respect for the dead. The Spanish also brought their own customs with them when they came to the New World. They combined traditions and called the celebration *El Dia de Los Muertos* (the Day of the Dead). It's not weird or scary—it's fun. It is a way for people to show respect for their dead relatives.

Some ideas behind this holiday come from the ancient Indians of the Americas.

For example, the Taino Indians of Cuba believed that at night their dead family members came back to their huts looking for food. So every night they would set out offerings of their favorite food for the relatives.

The Spanish explorers had a similar tradition they brought from their homeland. They had a special day they set aside to pray for people who had died. This day is called All Saints' Day, and it falls on November 1. The day after this was named All Souls' Day. It is a day when people pray for souls who haven't found a resting place. These ideas of paying respect to the dead were blended together and became the Day of the Dead.

The Day of the Dead was originally celebrated over three days. On the first day, living relatives go to their dead relatives' graves and set out candles and incense. They put flowers on the graves, especially marigolds because these flowers have such a strong, sweet smell. The relatives hope the dead can find their way home by following the smells of the flowers and incense, and the light of the candles. At home, they spend the day preparing all the food the dead person loved. They put the food on a table, and no one can eat it until the dead person is given enough time to have some.

On the second day, the families have big celebrations at their houses. They serve more of the dead person's favorite foods. Pictures, a favorite dress, or even objects that belonged to that person are set out to remind people that these dead relatives are present. They often eat candies shaped like skeletons and coffins. The skeleton is a very important symbol for this celebration because it is the last thing the dead relatives leave on Earth. Relatives and friends dance and sing and spend time remembering their dead loved ones.

On the third day, the celebration becomes more widespread. There are parades with floats and bands. Coffins are carried that have people in them dressed like skeletons. These skeletons first move their arms, then their shoulders, slowly coming out of the coffin to join the party. Americans celebrate some aspects of this three-day celebration in the form of Halloween. Halloween means "holy evening." This is often celebrated with festive foods and parties. Many costumes include skeletons and skulls. Some Christian religions have a special church service to remember their dead. Other Americans visit cemeteries or grave sites and leave flowers and flags on the graves to show love and respect for the dead.

CUSTOMS AND TRADITIONS

People of all ethnic groups have their own customs that have been handed down from generation to generation. Hispanic customs and traditions are a very important part of the culture.

Baptism

A baptism usually takes place just before a baby's first birthday. First of all, the parents of the baby have the important responsibility of picking godparents. Most of the time, the godparents' job is to give spiritual advice and guidance. Usually the godparents will buy the baptismal outfit for the baby, their new godchild (*ahijado*).

The baby's parents and godparents then become what's called compadres. Compadres are special friends that have a sacred bond between them. Usually gifts are given to the newly baptized baby. It is traditionally believed that giving the baby a piece of coral will bring good luck and protect the child from mal ojo—the evil eye. Many times the jewelry given to babies has a little piece of coral in it. For little girls, you might see coral on a baby bracelet or in their earrings. For little boys, the coral is usually hung somewhere in their crib.

Quinceanera

Navajo girls celebrate a Kinaalda, Jewish girls celebrate a Bat Mitzvah, and Hispanic girls sometimes celebrate a Quinceanera. A Quinceanera is a celebration that means the young lady is becoming an adult admitting her faith in God.

Quince in Spanish means 15, so a Quinceanera is celebrated around the girl's 15th birthday. Most Quinceaneras are fancy events, so lots of planning is needed. Just as a wedding does, a Quinceanera can take a year to plan.

For the celebration, the young lady must choose an escort for the day. She also chooses a Court of Honor (*Corte de Honor*) which is made up of pairs of boys

and girls. The boys are called Lords *(Chambelanes)* and girls are called Ladies *(Damas)*. The girl chooses 14 couples to represent each year of her life. She and her escort make the 15th year. Usually, the Court of Honor consists of relatives or close friends. All the Damas get together with the young lady to choose dress patterns and fabrics. Then they have to be fitted time and time again. The Chambelanes are lucky because all they have to do is rent their tuxes.

On the day of the Quinceanera, the young lady gets dressed in her fancy white dress and special necklace that her parents have bought her. Usually this dress looks like a wedding dress. It's white to represent her purity. The girl is driven to the church in a decorated car.

The ceremony begins like a wedding, with the 14 couples walking down the aisle followed by the young lady escorted by her parents. The first pew is reserved for the escorts. The boys sit on the right and girls on the left. During Mass, the girl rededicates her faith in the Catholic

Church. As a sign of faith, the girl will place either a single rose or a bouquet of roses beneath the picture or statue of the Virgin Mary. The girl and her parents are the first to receive Holy Communion. The rosary, Bible, and special necklace represent the connection between church and family. At the end of Mass, the young lady and her parents walk down the aisle with their arms linked together. Her escort, along with the Court of Honor, follows them.

Now comes the fun part. The guests usually arrive before the girl, her parents, her *padrinos* (godparents), her escort, and the Court of Honor. Sometimes a special archway is decorated for the Quinceanera party's entrance. First, the 14 couples go through the archway and make a long tunnel with their arms raised. Next, the young lady, her escort, the parents, and padrinos go through the archway and the tunnel. The 14 couples make a huge circle around them. The girl's mother gives the father a white satin pillow that has a pair of white high-heeled shoes on it. The father kneels on the satin pillow in front of the girl, slipping her old shoes off and placing the new ones on her feet. This is another symbol of the girl's move from childhood to adulthood.

Still in the circle, the young lady dances a special dance with her father while everyone else watches. During the dance, everyone helps themselves to food. Often the menu includes Mexican and American food in a buffet style.

Just as at any birthday party, the girl

receives gifts from her guests. The gifts vary from spiritual things to money, jewelry, or clothing. Like a wedding, a Quinceanera is a memorable event in any girl's life. Through a Quinceanera, a girl has begun her journey into womanhood.

In Mexico, boys celebrate Quinceaneros on their 15th birthdays. Quinceaneros are becoming more popular for boys here in the United States.

Wedding

Some people choose to get married by the justice of the peace. Others prefer a small church wedding. However, typical Hispanic weddings are famous for being large and fancy.

Traditionally, the bride's parents pay for the wedding, but today it's left up to the couple and their families. The bride and groom can also pick padrinos, or sponsors, for the wedding. (See the Quinceanera section for more about padrinos.) Padrinos can attend to many different parts of the wedding: the flowers, the cake, the cushions, the lazo, the candles, the rings, the music, the food, or even the videos.

Sometime during the ceremony, the priest or minister will ask for the *arras* (AH-rahs). The arras are 13 coins (sometimes gold-plated) that symbolize prosperity. The groom gives them to the bride, showing that he intends to always provide for her and their family. If the groom chooses to use regular coins, then they all must be the same kind of coin.

Next, the priest will ask for the *lazo* (LAH-zoh). The lazo is connected in the middle to form two loops. One loop is placed over the head of the bride, and the other is placed over the head of the groom. This takes place while they're kneeling right next to each other in front of the altar, to symbolize the two becoming one. Some lazos are very simple and made of rope, while others are fancy and made of satin or flowers.

The lighting of the candle is another important tradition. The bride and groom together light a big candle on the altar to symbolize the beautiful light of their glowing love in the eyes of God.

After the ceremony, there is a reception. The first dance at the reception is the traditional *marcha* (march). The marcha is lead by a couple that the bride and groom

have chosen. During the marcha, guests get up and join in at the end of the line. The marcha ends with the bride and groom dancing with their parents, padrinos, and finally, each other. You have to be in shape to dance the marcha because it usually goes on for about five to ten minutes.

FOOD

Hispanic cooking combines products and methods of two worlds. When the Spanish invaders came to the New World, they brought with them livestock, cheeses, orchard fruits, and wheat, along with their own ways of cooking. They met different native groups, such as the Mayas of Mexico or the Taino Indians of Puerto Rico. It's possible that some Spanish explorers forced the natives to use a Spanish style of cooking when they served

them. Eventually, these two heritages must have blended together, and a new way of cooking was invented.

Let's think about how this could happen. If your dad were cooking a recipe for your family, he might change it a little because he couldn't find one of the items in the recipe. Everyone might really like the new way he cooked the food, and now he has a new recipe. This is one of the reasons that recipes for the same Hispanic dish can be so different.

In discussing Hispanic food, we found out that all 82 authors in our writing program had eaten at a Hispanic restaurant. We all had tasted tacos and burritos served in our school cafeteria. We were all familiar with foods such as guacamole, enchiladas, salsa, and nachos. We also had a chance to make a few Hispanic dishes for this book. In the pages to follow, we've given recipes for the dishes we liked and think other kids can make. Ask your dad or mom if you can prepare some of our dishes. Read on to find recipes for drinks, appetizers, main dishes, and fruit popsicles.

Tortillas

A tortilla is a flat bread made from flour or corn. It can be stacked, rolled, folded, eaten alone, or eaten with other foods. You can buy machine-made tortillas in almost any American supermarket. We thought you might like to know how to make them.

Making tortilla dough

4½ cups flour
2 tbs. baking powder
1 tsp. salt or to taste
3 tbs. solid vegetable shortening
½ cup lukewarm water

Put flour in a big glass bowl. Then add salt, baking powder, and the vegetable shortening. Mix ingredients until the mixture looks like a rough rock. Add water slowly, and knead until the dough looks like a smooth ball. Cover with a towel and set aside for half an hour.

To make the tortillas, pinch out little balls of dough and put them on a cutting board that has flour lightly sprinkled on it. Then get a rolling pin and one ball of dough and roll it into a flat circle. Put the flat circles on a warm griddle. You have to cook each side until it's golden brown. Now you have great flour tortillas.

How to Fold a Tortilla for a Burrito
A burrito is a folded flour tortilla with different kinds of fixings in the middle, such as cheese, meat, vegetables, and salsa. Have you ever noticed that at Mexican restaurants, they fold their burritos in a fancy way? Well, here we're going to teach you how to do it.

First, place your meat and vegetables in a strip down the middle of your tortilla. Fold the bottom part of the tortilla over your filling, just enough so you can still see some of the meat. Fold in the sides, then the top part. Now you can eat your meal with a fork or with your hands.

Salsa para los Niños (Dip for Children)

Tired of plain old salsa? If you are, then try the following recipe. Salsa is a thick tomatoey sauce that can either be spicy or mild. Here's a recipe we liked. It makes 3 cups.

1   28-oz. can Italian-style
      tomatoes
¼   cup onions
½   tbs. vinegar
1   tbs. salad oil
1   tsp. finely crushed oregano leaves
1   tsp. finely crushed parsley leaves

Crush tomatoes by hand. Add the rest of the ingredients. This salsa is a mild sauce that most children like. Put it in a light-colored bowl so people will know it's mild.

This salsa is wonderful on tacos, burritos, nachos, corn chips, and most Mexican dishes. It's guaranteed to be a favorite.

Guacamole

3   large peeled avocados
½   cup chopped onion
1   cup chopped tomato
1   tbs. lime juice (to keep sauce
      from turning brown)

First cut up the avocados and put them in a pan or bowl. Save the seed in the middle for decoration when done. Then take the tomatoes and onions and spread them around the avocados. Mash all the ingredients together. After mashing the avocados, put the lime juice into the mixture and mix it one last time.

Huevos Rancheros

You need a frying pan and a stove to make this. Ingredients are eggs, oil, tortillas, and salsa. Put the frying pan on the stove and warm the oil in the frying pan. Get some eggs and crack them into the frying pan. Now fry the eggs. Put a tortilla on a plate, then put the eggs on the tortilla. Take some salsa and put it on top of the eggs. Roll up your tortilla.

Chorizo con Huevos (Scrambled Eggs and Mexican Sausage)

8   eggs
3–4   links chorizo sausage
      Garlic powder to taste

First peel off the skin of the chorizo. Next get a frying pan and mash the chorizo in the pan with a big spoon. Cook the chorizo with a little bit of oil. When done, drain all of the chorizo grease. Next put the eggs in the pan. Scramble the eggs, mixing in chorizo and the amount of garlic powder you want. Serve with a flour tortilla or a big piece of french bread.

Chicken Enchiladas

1   chicken, about 3 pounds
1   medium onion, chopped
3   tbs. butter
1   can cream of chicken soup
1   can cream of mushroom soup
1   cup chicken broth
1   4-oz. can green chiles, chopped
1   doz. corn tortillas
1   lb. longhorn cheese, shredded

Cook and bone chicken. Brown onion

Making bean dip

in butter. Add soups, broth, chiles, and chicken, and heat well. In a large deep pan, layer the tortillas, chicken sauce, and cheese. Repeat until the casserole is filled, ending with cheese. Bake 30 minutes at 350 degrees. Serves eight.

Arrachera al Carbon (Mexican Fajitas)

1 lb. trimmed skirt steak or chicken, cut into 3-inch lengths
1 onion per pound grilled with meat
1 green pepper per pound grilled with meat
1 lime per pound grilled with meat

3 sprigs of cilantro
Salt, pepper to taste

Squeeze lime juice over the meat. Grill on a charcoal grill. Serve with guacamole, tortillas, and lots of salsa. Serves four.

Atole de Fresa (Creamy Strawberry Breakfast Drink)

This drink is very smooth. It goes well with breakfast . This drink is very enjoyable on a cold day instead a cup of hot chocolate!

2 qts. fresh or frozen strawberries
½ cup white cornmeal substitute

½ cup all-purpose Cream of Wheat
or wheat flour
4 cups milk, scalded
2 cups water
1 cup sugar
1 tsp. vanilla
A few drops red food coloring
½ tsp. cinnamon

Squash the well-washed strawberries. Blend the white cornmeal with the water. Slowly add the sugar and stir for ten minutes. The mixture should be thick. Add the strawberries, vanilla, cinnamon, cream, and the few drops of food coloring. Heat until boiling begins, stirring every few minutes. Makes four quarts.

Chocolate Mexicano (Mexican Hot Chocolate)

When it's cold outside and you need something warm to drink, you might want to try this.

2 3-oz. cakes or tablets Mexican
chocolate (6 oz. sweet
cooking chocolate can be
used instead)
6 cups milk
2 tsp. cinnamon (if using
cooking chocolate)
2 tsp. sugar

Combine all the ingredients in a saucepan and cook over low heat. Stir constantly until the chocolate has melted and the mixture is blended. Just before serving, use an eggbeater and beat until smooth. Serves four.

Fruit Punch

This fruit punch is a delicious drink on a hot summer day.

¼ cup sugar
1 cup orange juice
4 cups grape juice
4 cups club soda
½ lemon, sliced
½ orange, sliced
1 small apple or peach, cut into thin
wedges
ice

Put the sugar, orange juice, and grape juice in a pitcher. Add the lemon, orange, and apple or peach slices. Stir the mixture until the sugar disappears. Just before you serve the drink, put in club soda. Add ice if you want.

Dancers from Our Lady of Guadalupe parish, Denver

Paletas
(Fruit Popsicles)

    2 cups sweet pureed fruit
    1 cup juice
    2 tbs. sugar
    ½ tsp. lime juice

Get the fruit you like and mash it. Then put it into a bowl. Add the fruit juice and mix together. Then add the sugar and lime juice to keep the color of the fruit. Put contents into two ice-cube trays. Stick toothpicks into the center of each cube. Freeze for 3 to 7 hours.

DANCES

What would a festival be like without dancing? Dancing is done all over the world. All cultures have some form of the art of dance. In fact, many anthropologists, people who study cultures, believe dance actually started when male animals wanted to attract female animals. They jumped around and looked beautiful so that the female animal would notice them. Dance was also used in many cultures to ask the gods for favors, such as rain, a new baby, or victory over a rival. In some cultures, only men dance, while in others,

Native American culture has influenced Hispanic dancing

only women dance. In the Hispanic culture, both men and women dance.

Dancing has many basic elements, such as steps, gestures, and rhythm. Dancing is made up of parts of people's movements, like walking, jumping, skipping, running, hopping, galloping, sliding, swaying, and turning. In ancient times, dancers often made their own music by singing, shouting, or clapping.

As dances became more involved, musicians started to provide music. Specific music was selected to go with certain dances. The basic rhythm of a dance is closely related to the music. Music and

dance belong together. They are both based on rhythm and movement. Dance can be used as an expression of our emotions, or it can help us feel a specific way. It has helped some religious people express their love for God. Dance can also be used to tell a story.

In the early 1800s, traditional Mexican folkloric dancing began. This type of dance is very important to the Hispanics because it expresses emotion and heritage. It is a blend of the Spanish, Indian, and Caribbean cultures. Folk dancing is handed down from one generation to the next. Many folk dances were made for pleasure. Some of these dances are for dating and have the dancers flirt with each other. The Cuban rumba is a dance that tells the story of a flirtatious exchange. The dancers move to show how boy meets girl, boy chases girl, and girl runs away. In a dance called "Bullfighting," the matador flirts with death.

Kids participate in traditional Mexican dancing

The styles of costumes for the dances have been passed down from generation to generation. For example, handmade Mexican costumes are chosen by color and expression for each dance. The dancers like to pick the colors for their costumes, unless they are for a group performance in which all costumes must match. The dresses usually have full skirts with lots of ruffles, lace, and ribbons. They are very long—almost to the ground—and make women look like big butterflies when they hold their dresses out to their sides. Men usually wear black suits with white shirts. The pant legs are tapered with rows of silver buttons down the outside of the leg. A sombrero (a wide brimmed hat) is the finishing touch on the men's costume. Some dancers use colorful scarves, castanets, and hand clapping.

The dance called "La Raspa"—meaning to scrape or scratch—is a Mexican folk dance consisting of an alternate shuffling of the feet forward and backward and ending with a pivot. This dance has specific music for its dance steps. Children often dance La Raspa at parties, birthdays, or just to feel good.

Some dances originated when Spanish music was mixed with the musical styles of blacks and Indians. The Mexican Hat Dance (*Jarabé Tapatío*) is a well-known Mexican dance. The Jarabé became known as the Mexican Hat Dance because

it's a dance performed around a hat. The boy dances on one side of the hat, and the girl dances on the other side. It's sort of a dance for boyfriends and girlfriends, because the dancers flirt with each other the entire time. The Jarabé Tapatío has always been a popular Mexican dance. It is frequently performed across America by the Ballet Folklorico Nacional. Many Hispanic communities across our country have Ballet Folklorico dance groups such as the ones in San Antonio, Texas, and Los Angeles, California.

Today in America, strolling musical groups called mariachis perform at street fairs and in restaurants. The mariachi groups have singers, musicians, and dancers. The dancers perform to lively music. They use a few basic steps, such as hopping, heel and toe tapping, and scratching. The musicians use all types of guitars, brass horns, and percussion instruments such as maracas and castanets.

Hispanic dancing is a world filled with history and tradition. It's a really good thing for kids to learn. In community churches and centers throughout America, there are many groups that hold classes to learn Hispanic dance. If you are interested in becoming a member of a dance group, contact Hispanic churches and centers to ask them about opportunities in your area. After students learn to dance, some perform in festivals and other celebrations. Learning Hispanic dancing is a great way to learn about the culture while having lots of fun!

There are many more Hispanic festivals, recipes, and customs to explore. We hope you are able to attend a Hispanic celebration or do your own investigating.

ART

Art has a great part in history.
It brings beauty to life's mystery.
The paint, the pen, the ordinary thing—
The joy and pain that art can bring.

As Americans across our country become more aware of taking care of our environment, American artists are starting to use recycled items in their art. This trend has been a part of Hispanic art for many years. Hispanic artists often use creativity to turn ordinary household stuff into beautiful, interesting pieces of art.

The artists discussed on the following pages create their art using Hispanic techniques. At the same time, they display their Hispanic heritage. Hispanics have come from Cuba, Mexico, Spain, Puerto Rico, and other places around the world. Where they come from makes their art different. For example, Cubans—who are islanders—might paint scenes of water. But Mexicans might paint mountains or land because they live in this type of area. Religion is an important part of Hispanic tradition, too,

and this religious heritage can be seen in Hispanic art. Artists use their feelings about family, saints, and Hispanic tradition to help them learn and share the beauty of the Hispanic culture.

Also in this chapter we will write about *retablos* [ray-TAH-blohs], *santos* [SAHN-tohs], and other types of folk art. Saints and other religious beliefs are used in this art, as are objects from everyday life. Some of this art is colorful, some is plain, but all of it is a beautiful expression of the artist's talents.

We also talk about piñatas, *luminarias*, and *molas* [MOH-lahs], three exciting art projects that you will be able to make. We have provided the directions and a list of materials for each activity at the end of this chapter.

Read on to find out about five Hispanic artists, three types of Hispanic art, and three art projects you might like to make at home.

ARTISTS

Consuelo Gonzalez Amezcua

Do you know which Hispanic artist's nick-name is "Chelo?" It was Consuelo Gonza-lez Amezcua. She was born in Mexico in 1903 and brought up in Del Rio, Texas. She was offered a scholarship to attend an art school, but wasn't able to go because of her father's death. She never went to school to learn art.

Instead, Chelo started drawing by doo-dling on her own. She used ordinary ball-point pens in red, blue, black, green, and purple, though not all of her drawings had color in them. Chelo also enjoyed paint-ing, but not as much as she enjoyed draw-ing. She called her style of drawing "Filigree Art: a new Texas culture." She takes three-dimensional designs and turns them into flat drawings. Because she didn't go to school, most of her art ideas came from the things she learned and saw at church.

Writing poetry is another of Chelo's inter-ests. She has won prizes for her poetry. Sometimes she even included poetry in her drawings.

Even though Consuelo Gonzalez Amezcua's family didn't always encourage her, she always knew she wanted to be an artist. Her designs and details amaze many of her admirers.

Carmen Lomas Garza

Carmen Lomas Garza is a talented artist who has shared her Hispanic heritage in her work. She was born in Kingsville, Texas,

in 1948. Carmen was the second child born in a family of five children. She went to a public school in Kingsville, and one thing she remembered from her childhood was getting spanked for speaking Spanish in class. Back then, speaking Spanish in school was against the law. Ms. Garza graduated from Texas Arts and Industries University in 1972.

Ms. Garza's mother was a florist, and her grandmother made paper flowers. Their artistic talents and projects helped Ms. Garza decide, when she was a teenager, to become an artist.

In college, Ms. Garza became involved in *El Movimiento*—the Chicano movement. Artists like Ms. Garza joined this movement because they were proud to be of Mexican descent. Their paintings showed a special pride in their heritage. A historian of the Chicano movement, Jacinto Quirarte, said that these artists enjoyed their work, not to be famous but "to teach the Chicano com-munity about itself, to strengthen it, and to nurture it." This means to learn more about yourself and to be proud of who you are. Ms. Garza wanted to help the community understand its heritage better.

Ms. Garza's paintings sometimes show His-panic people with their family. One of her paintings, called *Sandia Watermelon*, shows parents, children, and grandparents on the porch eating watermelon. Extended families living together (such as grandparents, aunts, uncles, grandchildren, and cousins) are important in the Hispanic culture. Another one of her famous pictures, done in 1977, is called *Death Cart*. This picture shows a

skeleton that could represent a part of the November 1 Day of the Dead celebration. (Read more about the Day of the Dead in the Fun, Food, and Festivals chapter.)

Another example of Ms. Garza's work is her *Homage to Frida Kahlo*, a famous Mexican artist who is an inspiration to many Mexican American women artists. Kahlo's paintings are like memories from a life— from someone who had a strong desire to paint despite her pain and suffering.

Ms. Garza now lives in San Francisco, California, and has had exhibits at the San Francisco Museum of Modern Art, the Mexican Museum of San Francisco, El Museo del Barrio (The Neighborhood Museum) of New York, and Intar Latin American Gallery of New York. Carmen Lomas Garza was recently featured in *Hispanic Art in the United States: Thirty Contemporary Painters and Sculptors* by John Beardsley and Jane Livingston. You might ask for this

book at your library, so you can see some photographs and examples of her work.

Eduardo Chavez

Eduardo Chavez was an interesting man. He was born in Wagon Mound, New Mexico, in 1917. Even though he went to Colorado Springs Fine Arts Center for a short time, he feels he taught himself to paint. Mr. Chavez featured American subjects in his murals, which are located in Glenwood Springs and Denver, Colorado; Geneva, Nebraska; Center, Texas; and Fort Warren, Wyoming. He has exhibited his work throughout Europe and Mexico.

When Mr. Chavez started his art career, he had two really good friends who one day died in a car accident. After his friends died, he made all blue paintings, because painters paint the things they feel. He used blue because it represents sad feelings. As time passed, Eduardo Chavez started to add more color to his paintings. Soon his paintings were more colorful and less sad. Today, his blue paintings are his most famous works of art. Our favorite painting of his is *Ocate 1*. It's very colorful. It has many shades of blue, and the colors seem to dance around all the other colors. This is a happy blue painting!

Octavio Medellin

Octavio Medellin is a Hispanic sculptor who is well known throughout Texas. He uses wood and stone to sculpt his wonderful statues and sculptures. He usually sculpts figures and animals that look strong and sturdy. They are huge and very heavy.

Mr. Medellin was born in Mexico in 1907. Living during the Mexican Revolution was not easy, and his family was forced to move many times. Finally they settled in San Antonio, Texas, in 1920. That is when he began to study art. He studied Indian crafts, which had a great influence on his sculptures. He also studied painting and life drawing. He tried to enroll in the San Carlos Academy of Mexico, but was not accepted because he didn't have enough schooling in art. He began sculpting in 1933. No one had ever taught him how to sculpt, so he is considered to be self-taught.

Mr. Medellin set up his very own gallery, the Villita, to help himself and other artists sell their artwork. After starting the art gallery, he taught for three years at two museums. It seems that you have to sell your art before anyone thinks you know enough to tell others about it. Sometime later, Syracuse University Library asked for his papers and art studies to put in its Collection of Manuscripts of Sculptors. After that, he began to run his own art school.

A lot of his sculptures have themes about history. One of Mr. Medellin's pieces is a great example of this living history. It is called *The History of Mexico*. On each side of it are carvings of things that happened at a certain time. These carvings tell a story to the viewer.

Since the late thirties, Octavio Medellin's art has been exhibited a lot, and he continues to make lifelike sculptures. He is a great sculptor because he uses ideas from his own mind and puts them into his many pieces of art.

Gregorio Marzan

Gregorio Marzan was born in 1906 in Puerto Rico. He attended school until he was nine years old, when he had to find a job. Mr. Marzan worked on the island of Puerto Rico as a carpenter and as a field hand. While he was working there, he got married and had five children. In 1937, he decided to move to New York City so he could find a better job. New York had many more job opportunities to help support his family. Sadly, his wife died before he got to New York. Eventually, when he could afford it, he brought his five kids, who had been living with their grandmother, to New York.

In New York, Mr. Marzan couldn't find a job as a carpenter, but he did find a job making toys, dolls, and stuffed animals. He worked in lots of toy factories until he retired in 1971.

During his retirement, Mr. Marzan started making small birds and houses typical of rural Puerto Rico to sell to gift shops. He tried to sell these home decorations to several gift shops, but they were not interested. When he was trying to sell his work to the gift shop at El Museo del Barrio, the museum director thought that his pieces were so good they belonged in the museum! This happened in 1979. The museum has been collecting his art pieces ever since.

Making recycled paper baskets

Gregorio Marzan does not think of himself as an artist, but he says he can make anything he sees. His ideas come to him when he is walking around, or they come from his memories of Puerto Rico. We like his work because it's very beautiful. For example, *The Dachshund* has a lot of glitter and parts of it look like shiny colored ribbon.

SOME TRADITIONAL HISPANIC ART FORMS

Retablos

Retablos are small, religious oil paintings. These paintings help others to see a picture of what a holy person such as Jesus or the Lady of Guadalupe (the Virgin Mary) might look like. They are usually painted on tin by untrained artists. Some artists use copper instead of tin for the retablos. The retablo was a favorite form of art in the early 1800s. Thousands of these holy pictures were painted during that time.

Santos

Later, some artists decided to carve saints and holy people out of wood instead of painting them on tin and copper. These works are called santos. They are three-dimensional, so you can walk around them. They are colorful, with reds, yellows, blues, greens, and browns. Black is sometimes used for outlines. Santos can be several inches or a few feet in height.

Folk Art

Artists also do folk art. We saw some that were three-dimensional. Folk art makes statements about things in the everyday lives of the Hispanic people. These events might include work, gardening, sports, church, or family activities. For Hispanic people, folk art is an expression of how they carry out everyday activities. It paints a clear picture of their community.

Folk art has changed a little from the colorful santos, but not very much. Today's folk artists want something new and different. They have less color compared to the retablos and the santos. Santos look more realistic than the retablo paintings. The folk art is plainer and doesn't have as many details. Folk art is usually made of natural wood so there is only the color of the wood.

The Hispanic people often use things like old cardboard and paper to write or draw on—even to make into new paper. They also use pieces of tin and copper and other materials to create sculptures. They use these leftover scraps to create interesting pieces of art. Something like an aluminum

can could be made into a colorful Christmas tree decoration.

FOLK ART PROJECTS

Piñatas

Making piñatas is an experience filled with history. Piñatas didn't start in Mexico. They started in Italy, and were first called *pignattas*. Back in the European Renaissance of the 14th and 15th centuries, pignattas were shaped like a clay ice cream cone. This cone shape was called a *pigna*. Later, the single cone became three cones put together like a star. The star symbolized the Three Kings and the gifts they brought

to baby Jesus at Christmas. Each point represents one of those Three Kings.

In 1498, on Columbus's third voyage, Father de Las Casas traveled as a Spanish missionary to Cuba. He showed the piñatas to the native people and told them how each point represented a king. Father de Las Casas saw how excited the natives were to find treasures and candies in the points of the star piñatas. He told them that if they became Christians, the Three Kings would fill the piñatas with candy and toys for all of them.

Mexico first used piñatas during the Feast of the Three Kings. Young children were told that the Three Kings were the ones

Materials: You will need one balloon, some thin newspaper strips, glue for making papier-mâché, three large rectangular pieces of paper, string, masking tape, tissue paper, and lots of cleanup supplies.

1. First, blow up your balloon.

2. Take the newspaper strips and pull them through the art glue that you have put into a small tub.

3. Next, make your pointer finger and your middle finger into a scissor form, and go down the strip. Be careful not to tear it. You do this so the glue doesn't glob up and look sloppy.

4. Now wrap your balloon with enough glued strips so that its color doesn't show through. Set your balloon to dry in the sun for about a day. Make sure it doesn't get dirty and that it doesn't drip on people.

5. Now you're ready to take the three rectangular pieces of paper and turn them into cones. You do this by holding the paper sideways with your thumb and pointer finger in the middle. Fold the paper toward the middle, being careful not to crease it. Do the same with the other side. Make sure there is a point at the top of the cone.

6. Do all of this with the three pieces of paper and tape the cone together so it doesn't unravel.

7. After that, tape these cones to the balloon so that it appears to be a three-pointed star when you look down on it.

8. Take the three pieces of string and tie them together so they look like a fat "Y." Now put the strings where they are

who put candy and toys in the piñatas. Children made their piñatas big because the bigger the star, the more gifts the kings would leave. At celebrations, they would hit the piñata with a stick, it would crack open, and the goodies would spill out.

Today, piñatas are fun for any party. They are smashing successes, literally. You can make a piñata, too! Here's how:

tied under the piñata. Bring them up in between the cones, and tie them together again at the top. Now you'll be able to hang up your piñata.

9. Then take the tissue paper and cut it into two-inch strips, the length of the paper. Fold the strips in half and cut the width of the strip to make a fringe. Be careful to keep it attached.

10. Take the side that's not fringed and put a thin line of glue on it.

11. Take the piñata, and start wrapping the tissue paper you just fringed around the tip at one cone. Make sure you cover the

Applying papier-mâché to a piñata

Making piñatas

newspaper. When you get to the center, wrap the strips in a circular motion, being careful to cover the top and bottom. If you missed a spot, you can use the extra tissue paper to patch it up.

12. If you want to, use any extra tissue paper as streamers. These are glued to the pointed ends of the piñata to make it more decorative.

13. Now you get to clean up! Let your piñata dry out by hanging it up somewhere. This also makes your room look festive—and you can even have fun while you're cleaning.

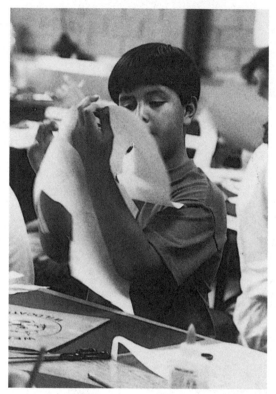

Making a mola

Molas

Molas are a colorful part of Hispanic culture. Their origin goes back to the Cuña Indians of Panama. A mola is a brightly colored geometric design. The Indians used shapes of living things like plants and animals for their designs. A mola is made of layers of the colored design placed one on top of the other. The Cuña Indians used fabric for their layers. They would put these layered shapes on a background and cover this background as much as possible. They could make them into pillows and blankets, and they even put the molas on their clothes. The Indians still make molas today. If you like the molas on the Indians' clothing, they may take them off and sell them to you.

Molas are fun to make. Many American tourists have brought these back from their visits to the Panama Canal area, and art teachers in American schools often have their students make molas as a Hispanic art project. They can be all sorts of colors and shapes, and you can start with any size you want.

This is a fun way to make molas:

Materials: Pencil, white paper, scissors, lots of colored construction paper, a large piece of white paper, and glue.

1. Draw a picture of your design on the white paper. You have to make all of the designs out of something in nature.
2. Cut it out with your scissors and trace your shape onto a piece of construction paper. Every time you cut it out, trace your shape bigger than the last one, and use a different color.
3. Then layer them from the biggest on the bottom to the littlest one on top.
4. After that, glue each design together.
5. Glue all of the designs on one large piece of paper covering as much of the paper as possible.

Molas are a great way to show something the ancient Cuña people did. Make one and hang it on the wall to show your friends.

Luminarias

Luminarias are lights set out along paths to lead the way on dark nights. During Las

Posadas, which are reenactments of when Joseph and Mary were looking for a place to stay, many people use luminarias to light the sidewalks and doorways to their homes. In America, luminarias are placed on houses and walkways around Christmas time to light the way for guests.

There are several kinds of luminarias. Often they are made using a brown bag with a candle inside. The type described here is made out of a tin can, using a hammer and nail to put in holes for a neat lighted effect that shines through the spaces. The designs are flashed across the walls and ceilings where the luminarias sit. *Materials:* Tin can, wood post, hammer, nails, can opener, paper, pencil, and your imagination. Use any kind of can, such as a

coffee can, bean can, or soup can. The can needs to be able to slip onto the round wood post.

1. Use your pencil and paper to make a repeating design something like this.

2. Get a tin can (like a small coffee can). Cut the ends out of the can with a can opener.

3. Tape your designs onto the tin can.

4. Take the wood post and stick it through the ends of the can.

5. Put the end of the posts on two tables or two chairs.

6. Use the hammer and nails to make holes for each dot on the design. Remember to pound the nail through the tin so that when you put the candle in the can, the light shines through.

7. When your design is done, remove the tape and paper design, put a candle inside, and place the luminaria in a dark place so that you can see how it works.

FUN WITH WORDS

Words! Words! Words!
Lots and lots of words.
Phrases, jokes, riddles, laughter—
Lots and lots of fun with words

We would like you to see how fascinating words are in English and Spanish. We hear both languages in many areas of the United States. This chapter will help you learn and understand *dichos* [DEE-chohs], *chistes* [CHEE-stehs] or *bromas* [BROH-mahs], *adivinanzas* [ah-dee-vee-NAHN-sahs], *palabras* [pah-LAH-brahs], Spanish place-names, *colores* [coh-LOH-rehs], and *frases* [FRAH-sehs].

DICHOS (Sayings)

Some dichos are passed on from generation to generation. They are sayings that you hear often. For example, *"Del dicho al hecho hay mucho trecho,"* which means "It's easier said than done." Sometimes dichos help you learn lessons or convince you to do something. They

are pieces of advice that will help you to avoid mistakes with people and in life. They will never grow old. Even though you can't always translate dichos literally, we picked out a few that we liked:

"Con la vara que midas, serás medido."
("With the rod that you measure, you will be measured.")

"Hablando del rey de Roma, mira quién se asoma."
("Speaking of the devil, look who's here.")

"El que no habla, dios no lo oye."
("If you don't speak up, you won't be heard.")

CHISTES (Jokes)

Chistes are jokes in question and answer form that make people laugh. They are

P: ¿Por que tienen los elefantes la piel arrugade?
R: Porque no se lo quitan para dormir!

Q: Why do elephants have wrinkled skin?
A: Because they don't take it off to sleep

also known as *bromas*. Some chistes are easier to understand in Spanish than in English. Sometimes it's hard to translate the punch line. Here are some chistes that we thought were especially funny.

SPANISH

Pregunta: *¿Por qué tienen los elefantes la piel arugada?*
Repuesta: *Porque no se lo quitan para dormir.*

ENGLISH

Question: Why do elephants have wrinkled skin?
Answer: Because they don't take it off to sleep.

SPANISH

P: *¿Por qué no dejo Caperucita Roja que el lobo se la comiera?*
R: *Porque no tenía permiso de su mamá.*

ENGLISH

Q: Why did Little Red Riding Hood not let the wolf eat her?
A: Because she didn't have permission from her mom.

SPANISH

P: *¿Por qué se fueron los cochinitos de su casa?*
R: *Porque su mamá era una cochina.*

ENGLISH

Q: Why did the piglets leave their house?
A: Because their mother was a pig.

SPANISH
Jorge: *¿Sabes que le dijo un olvidadizo a otro?*
Maria: *¿Qué?*
Jorge: *Ay, se me olvidó.*

ENGLISH
George: Do you know what one forgetful person said to another?
Maria: What?
George: Oops, I forgot.

ADIVINANZAS (Riddles)

Adivinanzas are riddles. They are similar to jokes, but longer. Sometimes they are confusing, funny, and mysterious. They often involve puns—words that sound alike, but have different meanings. When you try to translate adivinanzas from English to Spanish, they're not as funny. This is because in English, the similar words can't be used to mean the same as in Spanish. If you know someone who speaks Spanish, try to get them to tell the adivinanzas, because the humor is in the pronunciation. You have to use your mind to understand the answer, but it's funny even if you don't get it. However, we think jokes make you laugh harder than riddles.

SPANISH
Baila, pero no en la harina. ¿Qué es?

ENGLISH
She dances, but not in the flour. What is she?
Respuesta/Answer: *Bailarina* (dancer)
This combines the two words below.
(*baila*: dances) (*harina*: flour)

SPANISH
Una vieja larga y seca, que le escurre la manteca. ¿Qué es?

ENGLISH
A tall old woman, dried up stick, who drips
fat. Who is it?
Respuesta/Answer: *Una vela* (a candle)

SPANISH
Blanco como la nieve,
Prieto como el carbón,
Anda y no tiene pies,
Habla y no tiene boca. ¿Qué es?

ENGLISH
White as snow,
Black as coal,
It walks and has no feet,
It speaks and has no mouth. What is it?

Respuesta/Answer:
Una carta (a letter)

COGNATES

We thought you might enjoy some cognates.
Cognates are *palabras* (words) in Spanish
and English that come from the same root
word. They sound the same and have similar spellings and the same meanings. Here
are some cognates we thought of just for
you and just for fun. You might find these
words elsewhere in our book.

English	Spanish	Pronunciation
chocolate	*el chocolate*	[choh-coh-LAH-teh]
tomato	*el tomate*	[toh-MAH-teh]
boots	*las botas*	[BOH-tahs]
lemon	*el limón*	[lee-MOHN]
applaud	*aplaudir*	[ah-plah-oo-THEER]
rose	*la rosa*	[ROH-sah]
map	*el mapa*	[MAH-pah]
paper	*el papel*	[pah-PEHL]
music	*la música*	[MOO-see-cah]
musician	*el músico*	[MOO-see-coh]
bottle	*la botella*	[boh-TEH-yah]
cafeteria	*la cafetería*	[cah-feh-teh-REE-yah]
much	*mucho*	[MOO-choh]
salad	*la ensalada*	[ehn-sah-LAH-dah]
numbers	*los números*	[NEW-mehr-dohs]
colors	*los colores*	[coh-LOH-rehs]
vegetable	*el vegetal*	[veh-heh-TAHL]
explorer	*el explorador*	[ehks-ploh-rah-DOHR]
intelligent	*inteligente*	[een-teh-lee-HEHN-teh]

SPANISH PLACE-NAMES

Have you ever wondered why so many places in the southeastern and southwestern United States have Spanish names? It is estimated that more than 100,000 Spaniards came to the Western Hemisphere during the first half of the 16th century. When they came, they named many communities, rivers, areas, and settlements. Can you imagine if these places were called their English names instead of their Spanish ones?

Arizona (Arid Zone)
Colorado (Colored State)
Florida (Place of Flowers)
Montana (Mountain)
Rio Grande (Big River)
El Paso (The Pass)
San Antonio (Saint Anthony)
San Jose (Saint Joseph)
Santa Fe (Holy Faith)
Pueblo (Small Town)
San Francisco (Saint Francis)
Los Angeles (The Angels)
San Diego (Saint James)
Trinidad (Trinity)

   The next time you look at a map, try to see how many Spanish names you can find. Remember that many Spanish words end with a vowel. Also, Spanish names for places often include: *San* (male saint), *Santa* (holy, sacred; female saint), *Río* (river), and the words *los* or *las* (the).

LOS COLORES (Colors)

Here is a poem describing colors. We translated each color into Spanish.

I see red (*rojo*) as the fire at night.
I see the sky as blue (*azul*) and white (*blanco*).
I see brown (*café*) in coffee cups.
I see black (*negro*) spots on little pups.
I see green (*verde*) as stubby grass.
I see gray (*gris*) as swimming bass.
I see gold (*oro*) as the burning sun.
I see silver (*plata*) as a shining gun.
I see orange (*anaranjado*) as pumpkin seeds.
I see yellow (*amarillo*) in dandelion weeds.
I see pink (*rosado*) as a tie-dyed ant.
I see purple (*morado*) as a frozen eggplant.

No matter what color it is that we seek,
It makes no difference what language we speak.

FRASES (Phrases)

Here is a list of phrases that are easy to learn. You may want to use some of them the next time you are talking to a Hispanic friend. Or it might be fun to fool a friend by learning to say these Spanish sayings.

English	Spanish
Good morning	*Buenos días*
Good evening	*Buenas tardes*
Goodnight	*Buenas noches*
Good grief	*Qué barbaridad*
See you tomorrow	*Hasta mañana*
Hello	*Hola*
Good-bye	*Adiós*
How are you?	*¿Cómo está usted?*
Clean your room	*Limpia tu cuarto*
Be quiet!	*Callate!*
Get lost!	*Quítate de aqui!*
I love you	*Te amo*
Kiss me	*Bésame*
Thank you	*Gracias*
Please	*Por favor*
Excuse me	*Con permiso/Perdóneme*
You're welcome	*De nada*
What is your name?	*¿Cómo se llama?*
I'm lost. Can you help?	*Estoy perdido. ¿Me pueda ayudar?*
I don't speak Spanish	*No hablo español*
I don't know	*No se*
Merry Christmas	*Feliz Navidad*
Happy New Year	*Prospero Año Nuevo*

CUENTOS (Stories)

Stories are fun to hear,
Full of laughter and fear,
A word of wisdom for everyone,
A tradition of real Hispanic fun.

Storytelling is an important part of the Hispanic culture. Before there was even a written language, there was storytelling.

Stories were told not only as entertainment, but also as a way of teaching lessons and explaining why things were the way they are. They tell about a culture because they look at the morals and values of traditions and the lessons they teach. Every good story has something you can learn from it, even if it's just the idea that it's good to laugh.

Storytelling is an art. Not everyone is able to do it well. Storytellers tell their stories in the way they feel most comfortable with. No two storytellers tell the same story the same way. Storytellers use a lot of expression. They not only tell the story by using words but also by using all kinds of body movements. It's fun watching them as they move around while telling their stories. Many storytellers also use props such as hats, animals, other people, or musical instruments to add to their stories.

A famous saying among storytellers is, "I never let the facts get in the way of the truth." This means that although the message is usually true, the facts are sometimes exaggerated.

The best atmosphere for storytelling is a place with no distractions, a comfortable audience, and space to move around as you tell the story. If you want to be a successful storyteller, keep practicing—you might have the talent inside you. Find a story you like and practice telling it in front of a mirror, your pet, your friends, or on a tape. Keep your body moving. You may even be good enough to become a professional storyteller.

In this chapter, we share some of the

stories we've heard or read. Each contains a part of Hispanic culture, whether that part is funny, scary, true, religious, or romantic. We hope you enjoy reading them.

OUR LADY OF GUADALUPE

Do you believe in miracles? If not, then after you read this story you may think twice. If you already believe, then here's another one to add to your collection.

Most Americans have heard of Our Lady of Guadalupe. She is the patron saint of Mexico. Our Lady of Guadalupe has also appeared in places other than Mexico, and when she does, she takes on the nationality of that country. For example, she was called "Our Lady of Fátima" when she appeared at Fátima in Portugal. For these reasons, stories about the appearance of Mary have been carried on for many gen-

erations. Her popularity is shown by the large number of churches named after her in the United States. That is why we have included this story. It is a part of the past that will be shared by future generations.

In the year 1531, an amazing thing happened in the country now called Mexico. An Indian man named Juan Diego witnessed a miracle that changed his life forever. On his usual Saturday morning route to the church, Juan Diego heard beautiful music from the hillside of Tepeyac. He followed the sound to the top of the hill, where he saw a glistening white cloud with rays of rainbow colors all around. Coming closer, he heard his name being called. Suddenly the cloud split apart, and there before him stood a woman who looked like a beautiful Aztec princess. Instantly, he knew she was a saint, and he fell to his knees in praise.

The woman spoke very softly, saying, "I am the Mother of God, and I have come to give you an important message. Go to the bishop of Mexico and tell him I wish to have a church built in my name, here on this hill, to show my love for all my people."

Juan Diego told her, "I shall do as you wish." He ran as fast as he could to the bishop's house where he had to wait in line for a long time. Finally, one of the bishop's helpers asked Juan Diego why he wanted to see the bishop. Juan told his story to the bishop, who wasn't sure if he should believe him. He told Juan Diego to come back in a few days to give him time to think.

Juan went back to Mary, the Mother of God, and told her he was sorry, but he had failed. The bishop had not believed him.

Mary told Juan to go back to the bishop and demand that he build a church on that spot.

Juan returned to the bishop's house in hopes that he would be believed this time. He again had to wait to see the bishop. When Juan saw the bishop, he was not greeted warmly. The bishop told Juan to go back to the Lady and ask her for some kind of proof that the vision was real. Juan rushed back to the hilltop and gave Mary the news. She told Juan to return the next morning for the sign.

When Juan returned home, he found that his uncle was very ill and close to death. All night they tried different remedies to cure him. Nothing seemed to work, so Juan

was sent to fetch the priest to give his uncle his last blessings. On the way, he saw the Lady and told her why he couldn't meet with her. She told him not to worry because his uncle had been cured. She then told him to go to the top of the hill, gather some roses, and bring them back to her. Juan was puzzled because he knew no roses ever grew on the hilltop, especially in winter. But since he believed in the Lady, he went anyway. At the top of the hill he found a garden of beautiful roses. They still had dew-drops on them. He collected as many as he could hold in his cloak and returned to the Lady. The Lady tied his cloak around his neck and gently arranged the roses in it. She told him to take this sign to the bishop but not to show it to anyone else.

Juan took the roses and went swiftly but carefully to the bishop's home. He had to wait in line for the third time. The guards tried to get Juan to show them what he was hiding. Juan forgot his promise and showed the guards a small glimpse. Every time they would try to touch a rose, it disappeared into the cloth of the cloak. Not knowing what to do, they rushed him in to see the bishop. While in the bishop's private study, Juan opened his cloak and let the roses fall to the floor. Then he noticed that everyone was looking at his cloak. Juan looked down at it and saw a beautiful painting of the Lady. The bishop fell to his knees in prayer. The cloak was paraded around town so everyone could witness the great miracle. Soon a small church was built just as the Lady had requested. Years later, a beautiful cathedral was built in its place and

named *La Virgen de Guadalupe* (The Virgin of Guadalupe). In this cathedral hangs the actual cloak that Juan Diego wore. Even though it is more than 400 years old, it shows no signs of falling apart. This made believers out of us.

LA LLORONA
(The Weeping Woman)

Have you heard of the "Boogeyman"? In the Hispanic culture, the Boogeyman is known as La Llorona. She is feared by many children, and adults use her story as a warning to behave your best.

Once in a small Indian village, there was a girl named Maria. She was the prettiest girl in the village. She swore she would marry the most handsome man. Her *abuela* (grandmother) said that she should marry a good man and not worry about his looks. Maria didn't pay any attention. She wanted to marry a good-looking man. One day Maria saw a man come to the village. She thought that he was very handsome and asked him his name. He said his name was Gregorio. In about one month, they decided to get married. They had two kids after the marriage. The marriage worked for the first couple of years, but then things fell apart.

Gregorio started to see other women in front of his wife. He would take his girlfriend to visit his kids at home. He wouldn't even talk to Maria. He just ignored her.

Maria realized that her husband didn't care for her. He only cared for the kids. Soon Maria got jealous of her kids. She got very angry at her husband. She took her kids to the river and drowned them. Maria did this because she thought her husband would love her more without the kids around. When Maria got home, her husband just became angrier. Maria realized what she had done. She went back to the river and began running along the riverbank looking for her children. Paying more attention to the river instead of looking where she was going, she tripped over a root, fell right into the river, smashed her head on a rock, and drowned.

Two days later, they found her body by the riverbank. The town priest wouldn't let her be buried in the church graveyard because she had killed her kids. He said to bury her by the river. To this day, people swear they can hear her spirit

late and they should go home. Pablo said, "Why go home? We're having fun." They said La Llorona would get them if they didn't go home. They left, but Pablo stayed because he didn't believe the legend.

Soon it got dark and windy. Pablo started to see a white shadow coming through the trees. It sounded like a ghost. Pablo tried to run, but he couldn't. A voice started saying, *"¿Dondé están mis niños?"* ("Where are my children?") Pablo suddenly saw a white ghost flapping through the wind. The ghost—La Llorona—grabbed him, thinking he was her child. Suddenly, she heard the bell for Mass and disappeared in the trees. Pablo ran home as quickly as he could.

crying for her children by rivers and lakes. If she sees children, she picks them up and takes them away because she thinks they are hers. Parents tell their children that if they aren't good or don't come home on time, La Llorona will come and get them.

There is a story of Pablo who didn't believe in La Llorona. One day Pablo was playing by the river with his friends. Pablo's friends said it was starting to get

When he got home, his mom was mad at him for not coming home on time. He said, fearfully, "*Mamá*, La Llorona!" She didn't believe him and was ready to give him a good shaking when she saw on his shirt five red stains of blood left by La Llorona's fingers. Pablo's mom said that the story of La Llorona was true. So she got all the kids in the village and told them that when it gets dark, you better get home or La Llorona will get you.

This is one of the many versions of La Llorona. We think the original version was told during the time of Hernán Cortés.

EL GRILLO (The Cricket)

Many stories have a hidden moral or message. In this story, the message deals with stretching the truth. It's easy to exaggerate, but a story like this helps remind us how important it is to tell the truth.

In New Mexico, there once lived two men who were neighbors as well as *compadres* (godfathers to each other's children). One of the men was wealthy, hardworking, and well respected. The other was poor because he was lazy and didn't like to work at all. He had the nickname "The Cricket," because he talked and talked and was never quiet—like a cricket at night when you're trying to sleep.

The Cricket would brag that he was an *adivino* (fortune-teller) with special powers. Whenever the Cricket would get behind on paying his bills, he would take the rich neighbor's prize-winning mule and hide him in the mountains. His neighbor would come to the Cricket and beg him to use his special powers to find his prize-winning mule. The Cricket would pretend to see a vision. He would tell his compadre where his mule could be found, and—lo and behold—the mule would be there. The neighbor was so grateful to the Cricket that he would pay all his bills. This happened many times over the years.

One day, the rich neighbor was having lunch with the governor of New Mexico. The governor mentioned to his guest that he had lost his ring. The rich man bragged that his compadre was an adivino and could easily find the governor's ring. The governor didn't believe in adivinos, but thought it was worth a try. The Cricket was called before the governor. He tried to get out of the situation by denying he had magical powers. He said that he had been lucky once in a while. The governor got suspicious and decided to put the Cricket to the test. He locked him in a room and gave him three days to find his missing ring. If he was able to tell him where the ring was, he would be richly rewarded. But if he wasn't able to find the ring, he would be properly punished.

But the ring wasn't lost. It had been stolen by three of the governor's servants. They had it hidden in a safe place until they could sell it and split the money among the three of them.

All day, the Cricket sat next to the window watching the sun rise and set. He tried to think of a way to get out of the situation. At the end of the first day, one of the bad servants brought the Cricket his supper tray. He set the tray next to the Cricket and started walking toward the door. When the Cricket saw his supper tray, he realized that one of his three days had run out. "Of the three, there goes the first," he cried aloud. The servant thought the Cricket was talking about the three servants and not the three days. He ran down to tell the other two servants that the Cricket was truly an adivino. The other two servants tried to convince the first servant there was no such thing as an adivino.

The next evening, a different servant brought the Cricket's supper tray. The Cricket—thinking of the days again—said out loud, "Of the three, there goes the second." The second servant ran down the stairs and told the others that the Cricket knew all about them—he really was an adivino.

On the third evening, the last servant didn't even wait for the Cricket to say anything. He put down the supper tray, fell to his knees, and started confessing. He asked the Cricket not to tell on them. They would do anything he asked. When he heard the confession, the Cricket caught on right away. He told the servant he wouldn't tell if he would take the ring and make sure the governor's fattest goose swallowed it.

When questioned by the governor, the Cricket acted as if he had seen a vision. He told the governor that he had seen the ring inside the stomach of his fattest goose. The governor didn't believe him, but he decided to give the Cricket a chance. When they opened the goose's stomach, he was shocked to see the ring.

He rewarded the Cricket with a bag of gold and the goose to cook.

A few weeks later, the governor of Chihuahua, Mexico, was talking to the governor of New Mexico. The New Mexican governor bragged that in his state, there lived a real adivino. The two men began arguing about the truth of adivinos. They finally ended up betting $1,000 on whether the Cricket was a fake or not. The governor of Chihuahua said he would put something in a box and raise it to the top of the flagpole. The Cricket would have to tell what was in the box. If he couldn't, the governor of New Mexico would have to pay $1,000 to the governor of Chihuahua. If he could, then it was the other way around.

The governor of Chihuahua decided to try to trick the Cricket. He took a big box and put a smaller box inside it, then put a smaller box in that one, and so on, until he had a tiny box. He went out into the garden to find something small. Just then, a cricket hopped across the path. He picked up the cricket, put it inside the smallest box, sealed it, and had it pulled up to the top of the flagpole.

The Cricket was brought forth to settle the bet. There was no way for him to escape, because the governor of Chihuahua stood on one side and the governor of New Mexico stood on the other. A circle of soldiers surrounded all three of them.

Cricket stood there speechless, looking up at the box. An hour passed, then two hours. Finally, the governor of Chihuahua started to chuckle, so the governor of New Mexico got mad and said, "Tell us what's in the box in one minute—or I'll have your head!"

The Cricket started to stutter, "In the box . . . um, in the box . . . in the box . . ." The governor of Chihuahua was astonished. He thought the Cricket could see there was a box inside a box inside a box. Finally, the Cricket, only thinking of himself, moaned, "Oh, you poor Cricket, they've got you now!" When they opened the box, the governors, of course, found the little cricket in the last box. The governor of Chihuahua handed the money to the governor of New Mexico and became a believer. The governor of New Mexico was so pleased that he gave half the money to the Cricket.

While walking home, the Cricket promised never to tell anyone he was an adivino ever again. He soon came upon the neighborhood kids who always teased him. They had filled a sack full of trash and asked him to use his special powers to see what was in the bag. The Cricket was angry, so he yelled, "Leave me alone—that's just a bunch of garbage!" That comment made believers out of the boys. They spread the news, and soon everyone within miles called on the Cricket to find anything they had lost. The Cricket got tired of always being called on, so he moved to someplace where nobody had ever heard of an adivino.

LOS RATONCITOS
(The Little Mice)

This story about a mouse family is short but has a very important message. We chose it because this message is important for all Americans. See if you can guess what the mother mouse teaches her children.

There once was a mother mouse who had four children. The baby mice were so young that they had never been outside before. One day, they climbed all the way up the hole to see what they were missing. They smelled the air, which was very fresh. They went down the hole and asked their mom if they could take a walk.

She thought it was a wonderful idea, so she led them up the hole and through the grass. Just then, they heard, "Meow, hiss, meow, hiss!" It was *el gato*—the

Ratoncitos

cat! She told her children to run. They all ran and hid. The mother knew she had to protect her children, so she looked the cat in the eye, stood as tall as she could, and while shaking her fist said, "Ruff, Ruff, Ruff, Ruff!" The cat got scared by the sound of the barking dog and ran away. The mother mouse told her children to come out. She said to them, "It always helps to know a second language."

EL PRINCIPE Y LOS PAJAROS
(The Prince and the Birds)

Once there was a Spanish prince whose father locked him in his room. The only two people who came to see him were his father and his tutor.

One day, a dove flew onto his windowsill. The prince fed him bread and water, then put him in a golden cage. The next day, the prince saw the dove crying and asked him what was wrong. The dove told him he wanted to see his loved one. The prince asked the bird what a loved one was. The bird said a loved one was somebody who comforts you. The prince opened the cage and let the bird fly back home.

The next day, the dove came back and told him of a beautiful princess. The dove was sorry he couldn't take the prince on his back, but he suggested writing a letter. In a couple of days, the bird came back, half dead, with an arrow through his heart and a locket around his neck. The prince opened the locket, and there was a picture of the princess. He decided he would set out to find the princess. So the prince smashed the lock on his door and went to look for the princess.

On the way, the prince ran into some birds who helped him. Phoo was one of them. Phoo said, "Go to the castle." The prince went to the castle and saw a parrot. The parrot took the prince to see a raven. The raven told him about love.

They went to a castle in a different town, where the princess lived. The parrot went to the princess and told her the prince had come. She told the bird to take her scarf and tell the prince there would be a tournament and she was the prize. The prince was scared because he didn't have any equipment to fight with.

Just then, a stork came. He took the prince and the parrot to his cave. He showed him weapons and shields to use in the fight. The next day, the prince prepared for the tournament. He knew he wouldn't be allowed in the tournament, because the king knew the prince was the only one who could beat him. The king ordered his guard to keep the prince out of the tournament. He didn't want his daughter to marry anyone. The prince killed the guard to get into the tournament. He defeated all the other suitors. Finally, it was the king's turn to fight the prince. The princess fainted because she was afraid her father—or her prince—might die. When the princess didn't wake up, the king hired people to try to heal her.

One day, the prince dressed up as a wizard and went to the princess. He read her the poems he had written. She woke up. They stepped onto his magic robe and flew away together. They lived happily ever after.

THE LEGEND OF EL SANTO NIÑO

Have you ever heard of the legend of *El Santo Niño* (The Holy Child)? Many people call it a miracle. There are different versions of "El Santo Niño" throughout the Hispanic culture. We would like to tell you about two of the more famous versions. One happened during the eighth century,

and one continues to happen right now in the United States.

The first is the legend of El Santo Niño de Atocha. During the Muslim occupation of Spain in the eighth century, Catholic heads of families were thrown into prison. Once they were in prison, they often weren't given any food or water. There was nothing for their families to do but to pray for help. The only people who were allowed to visit the prisoners were small children.

One night, a little boy dressed as a pilgrim made the rounds of the prisons in the city of Atocha. In his hands he carried a small gourd of water and a basket of bread for the prisoners. He went to every dungeon and fed every prisoner, saying a blessing over each one. Guards were astonished to see that when the little boy left the dungeon, his basket and gourd still contained bread and water, even though he had fed so many prisoners. His miraculous supply was bottomless.

Many believe this little child was Christ. It's wonderful to know that this miracle happened, but it's even more wonderful to know that the spirit of El Santo Niño still continues to perform miracles today. An example of this is the story of El Santo Niño de Chimayó.

Many people visit an old church near Taos, New Mexico, to pray for help from El Santo Niño de Chimayó. Because the holy child is known to help sick children. many parents take their sick children to Chimayó. In the back of the church is a hole in the ground filled with dirt. Some people say that if you rub the dirt on a sick or crippled child, he or she will soon be cured. If you visit this famous place, you'll see crutches and braces that have been left there by children who have been cured and no longer need them. Some people also believe that El Santo Niño walks at night, healing sick children.

It's nice to know that good things still happen in our world. Maybe you can visit this special little church someday.

If you like these stories, check in your local library, your school or university libraries, or any bookstore for more. Here are just a few suggestions:

The Silver Whistle, by Ann Tompert, illustrated by Beth Peck (New York: Macmillan Publishing Co., 1988). This is a beautiful story about a Mexican boy who gives a special gift to the Christ child.

The Day It Snowed Tortillas, retold by Joe Hayes, illustrated by Lucy Jelinek (Santa Fe: Mariposa Publishing, 1990). This book has many folktales from Spanish New Mexico. There's bound to be one you like.

The Lady of Guadalupe, written and illustrated by Tomie de Paola (Holiday House, 1980). This is the story of how Our Lady of Guadalupe became the patron saint of Mexico.

Pedro and the Padre, by Verna Aardema, illustrated by Friso Henstra (New York: Dial Books, 1991). This is a story that teaches a lesson about telling lies.

FAMOUS FIRSTS AND HEROES

We call these people heroes,
Because they do their best.
They are making a difference,
As they try to help the rest.

This chapter tells the stories of well-known—and not so well-known—Hispanic Americans. All of them have worked hard to learn their special skills. When they faced hard times, they kept on going. They showed their courage and determination. They were devoted to reaching their goal.

Many of the people we've written about are the first Hispanics to do something important in their field. Others are heroes who have always tried to make the best of themselves and bring out the best in others. You will learn that people can make a difference in this world. These "famous firsts and heroes" have made the world a better place.

One thing we discovered about famous Hispanics was that sometimes they had to deal with a lot of prejudice. In the past,

they often changed their names to English names so that they would be able to fit in with everyone else. Two people who did this were Martin Sheen and Ritchie Valens. Martin Sheen's real name is Ramon Estevez and Ritchie Valens' real name was Richard Valenzuela. Their agents told them then that if they wanted to be big in the U.S., they would have to change their names. Today, most Hispanics are keeping their real names.

In this chapter, we were able to tell you about only a few of the Hispanics that have served in the military. You'll read that many received high honors. Together, Hispanic Americans won more medals than any other minority group in World War II. One example of a military hero is Private José P. Martinez. He was part of the Seventh Army Division that fought in World War II. He won the Congressional Medal of

Honor for saving the lives of the men in his unit in a battle in Japan. We visited his statue while writing this book. He was a true hero.

Many Hispanics have also made a difference in politics. Lauro Cavazos became the first Hispanic Secretary of Education. Manuel Lujan was the first Hispanic Secretary of the Interior. Ilena Ros-Lehtinen became the U.S. representative from Florida, and Rebecca Vigil-Giron was New Mexico's secretary of state. Jose Serrano from New York State and Dan Morales from Texas, were representatives in their states' governments. Jerry Apodaca of New Mexico and Raul Castro of Arizona both became governors of their states.

Famous Hispanic Americans can also be found in the sports world. Tom Flores started as a quarterback for several NFL teams before becoming a head coach for the Los Angeles Raiders and the head coach and general manager of the Seattle Seahawks. Lou Piniella became the manager of the Cincinnati Reds. Jose Torres, a former world champion boxer, became the New York Commissioner of Boxing. Ron Rivera was a professional football player for the Chicago Bears. Max Montoya and Anthony Munoz became great National Football League stars. The three Zendejas brothers (Luis, Max, and Tony) all kicked for NFL teams. Jose Canseco and Ruben Sierra are just two of the many Hispanics who have done extremely well in professional baseball in the U.S.

Some Hispanics have also won gold medals in the Olympics. Arlene Limas won a gold medal in tae kwon do, a type of martial arts. Tino Martinez and Robin Ventura have both won awards in baseball, and Joe Vigil became an Olympic track coach.

Read on to learn about more civil rights leaders, inventors, scientists, doctors, educators, religious leaders, people in government, explorers, athletes, entertainers, performers, and others. Some of these people are famous. Others you won't know. Many of the more famous Hispanic Americans were left out because you can find books in the library about them. You'll find some Hispanic artists in the Art chapter. We hope you will go to the library and read more about great Hispanic Americans.

As you read their stories, remember that if it hadn't been for these famous people, our world would be quite different than it is today. Even though some have died, their message lives on in our hearts. If we learn from them, we too can make the world a better place.

Father Junípero Serra (1713–1784)

Did you know that Junípero Serra was a priest and that his real name was Miguel Jose Serra? He was born on November 24, 1713, on an island named Mallorca in the Mediterranean Sea. He wasn't very healthy, and everyone thought he was going to die, so they baptized him right away. A lot of time went by, and he did not die. In fact, he lived more than 70 years. Miguel was a bright child. He was always happy and had a wonderful singing voice. Some people

said he sounded like an angel when he sang in the choir at school. As he grew up, he always enjoyed listening to stories of the New World.

As a boy, Father Serra was sent to Spain to study at a university because he was a great student. When he was 16, he joined the Order of Saint Francis—a Catholic group started by St. Francis that helps the poor. Miguel Serra changed his first name to Junípero because that was the name of one of Saint Francis' loyal friends. He taught at the university for many years after he graduated.

Father Serra never forgot the stories about the New World he heard as a boy. He decided to go to Mexico to work, because he heard there were people there who had never heard about Jesus. He wanted to tell them about the Gospels and help make

the world a better place. He left with Father Palou and sailed for 100 days to get from Spain to a port in Mexico called Veracruz. The priests set off immediately for the College of San Fernando in Mexico City. He taught there for several years. Then Father Serra formed a team to set up missions along the coast of California.

Father Serra was a kind man. He worked with Native Americans and treated them with respect. When Father Serra arrived at a village, he would hang a church bell and ring it to bring people together to talk about Jesus. His first mission was founded in San Diego in 1769. He also started eight more missions along the coast of California. Many of the mission buildings are still standing today and are some of the oldest buildings in the United States. He traveled back and forth to all the missions, even though he wasn't healthy. He died in his mission at San Carlos on August 28, 1784. He was made a saint by the Catholic Church on September 25, 1988.

Loreta Janeta Velazquez (1842–1893)

In 1842, Loreta Janeta Velazquez was born in Cuba. Her parents were Spanish. Loreta was 14 years old when she ran off to get married to a U.S. Army officer. When her husband left to serve in the army, she kissed him good-bye. Loreta wanted to be a soldier even more than her husband.

Loreta Velazquez didn't care about doing what others told her she should do. She wanted to fight in the Civil War. She went to New Orleans and found a tailor who would make her a uniform and wouldn't tell anyone what she wanted to do. Her husband was killed accidentally while loading his gun. Loreta realized that she was completely alone and would be able to take his place in the army. She joined the Confederate Army. Everyone knew her as Lieutenant Harry Buford—a man.

In 1861, Loreta Velazquez fought in the Battle of Bull Run. She fought in the Battle of Shiloh in 1862. Loreta Velazquez liked adventure, and that's what she found when she became the only woman to go into the army more than 100 years ago.

Juan Guiteras (1852–1925)

Juan Guiteras was born in Cuba in 1852. When he was 16 years old, his family moved to the United States.

Juan went to the University of Pennsylvania to become a medical doctor. He wanted to study yellow fever in order to help people living in Cuba. He and another doctor learned how mosquitoes spread yellow fever. When they made this discovery, it became easier for other doctors to find a cure for the disease.

Later, he became a teacher at the medical school. Dr. Juan Guiteras helped save many lives.

Diego Rivera (1886–1957)

Did you know that Diego Rivera was a famous painter? Years ago, no one owned televisions. Diego painted murals for the people so they would learn about their country's current and past events. His parents sent him to art school to study sculpture, but he liked painting better. He painted everything he saw.

Diego Rivera was born December 8, 1886, in Mexico. His mother didn't have a happy life because his twin brother became sick and died. Then little Diego got sick, too. The doctor said he needed a nurse. His family found someone to care for him. Her name was Antonia and she was an Indian doctor. Antonia took Diego to her tiny cabin in the mountains. He loved it. During the day, he would play in the forest, and he soon became strong and healthy. When it was time to go back home, his parents gave him a welcome-home present of colored chalk. Diego started drawing everywhere—even on the walls. He enjoyed drawing so much that his parents built him an art shop.

School was hard for young Diego. He would daydream throughout the day. He liked going to church to see the pictures in the squares on the wall. Finally, his parents sent him off to art school, but art school was boring for him. He didn't want to draw models, he wanted to paint real life scenes.

Later, Mr. Rivera went to Italy. He saw pretty murals inside the churches. He used these ideas when he went home to paint. This is how he began painting murals, which are pictures on walls. This made him famous throughout the world. His murals tell of his Mexican heritage and make people proud to be Mexican.

Mr. Rivera expressed his concern for humankind in his art. He made art his life. He wanted to do something for his friends and family, so he wrote a book that told his life story. Diego Rivera died while he was working in his art shop.

We are glad people can still see his murals everywhere, including Michigan, California, Mexico, and in many other countries around the world.

Dennis Chavez (1888–1962)

How would you like to be the first Hispanic U.S. senator? Dennis Chavez was a senator for 27 years, because he was reelected four times. He was a strong supporter of civil rights, and a United States stamp was recently printed with his picture on it.

Dennis was born to a poor family in a small village near Albuquerque, New Mexico. He was the third oldest of eight kids in his family. They moved to Albuquerque when he was seven and went to school there. He dropped out of school in eighth grade because his family needed him to work. He helped support his family for the next five years by driving a grocery wagon. School was very important to him, so he went to the public library to study.

Mr. Chavez never finished high school, but he passed a special test that allowed him to attend college. He went to Georgetown University. In 1920, he earned a law degree.

In New Mexico, Mr. Chavez opened a law practice and ran for public office. He became a U.S. representative in 1930. In 1935, he became a senator. One of his accomplishments while in office was to write a bill for the federal Fair Employment Practices Commission.

Mr. Chavez did many great things for Hispanic Americans and the rest of the nation.

Luis Alvarez (1911–1988)

Do you know how the dinosaurs disappeared? Luis Alvarez—a Nobel Prize winner—and his son wrote an article about how the dinosaurs might have disappeared.

Luis Alvarez was born in 1911 in San Francisco, California. The Alvarez family came to the United States from Cuba and had a long history of being scientists. Luis' grandfather was a doctor in Hawaii before it became a state, and his father was a doctor at the famous Mayo Clinic. Luis became a doctor, too, and today his son Walter is an important geologist.

Luis went to school in Rochester, Minnesota. Then he went to the University of Chicago to study a kind of science called physics. After he graduated, he became a professor at the University of California. That's where he helped develop a radar beam for airplanes that lets pilots land a plane even if they can't see the ground. This technology is still used today.

During World War II, Dr. Alvarez worked on the atom bomb. He watched the first atomic bomb explode on Hiroshima, Japan, on August 6, 1945. He was on a plane with other scientists behind the plane that dropped the bomb. That same night, he wrote a letter to his young son that said he "hoped that this terrible weapon we have created may bring countries of the world together and prevent further wars."

Dr. Alvarez won the Nobel Prize for physics in 1968 because he developed a hydrogen bubble chamber. It was a very important and powerful instrument that helped scientists learn a lot of things.

Walter Alvarez, Dr. Alvarez's son, is an important geologist who has an interesting idea about how the dinosaurs disappeared. Walter and his father wrote an article that described Walter's ideas. He believes that 65 million years ago, a giant rock from space hit the Earth. Lots of dust went into the air and blocked out the sun. Because plants can't grow without light, the plants died. The plant-eating dinosaurs eventually starved to death. This is called the "impact theory." What do you think?

Hector Garcia (b. 1914)

Many Mexican Americans fought bravely in World War II and made our country proud. But instead of coming home from war and being treated like heroes for their accomplishments, many were humiliated because of their heritage.

Hector Garcia was born in Mexico on January 17, 1914. He grew up in Mercedes, Texas, with parents who taught him to be proud of his heritage. After his brother graduated from medical school and became a doctor, Hector decided he'd give it a try. He hoped to become a doctor like his brother. So he went to the University of Texas Medical School, and became a doctor in 1942. Dr. Garcia joined the army during World War II, and received the Bronze Star Medal for his service.

After the war was over, Dr. Garcia heard about unkind things that had happened to many Hispanic GIs. He became angry. When he heard the stories of Macario Garcia and Felix Longoria, he decided to fight for the constitutional rights of people of Hispanic heritage.

After World War II, Macario Garcia was awarded the Congressional Medal of Honor, the highest and most important award a soldier can get in the military. At home in Texas, he went into a coffee shop to get some coffee. The owner told him that he didn't serve Mexicans. Mr. Garcia said, "If I'm good enough to fight your war for you, I'm good enough for you to serve me a cup of coffee." The owner grabbed him and tried to throw him out the door. Mr. Garcia was put in jail.

Felix Longoria never came home from World War II because he was killed during a battle. When his body was sent home to be buried, a Texas undertaker wouldn't bury it. President Truman was upset by this, so he had Mr. Longoria's body buried in Arlington National Cemetery in Washington, D.C.

Dr. Garcia decided that he couldn't let these kinds of things happen anymore. So on March 26, 1948, he started the American G.I. Forum, a group of Hispanic servicemen that worked to get back their rights as American veterans. By the 1950s, G.I. Forum members were all around the United States. The G.I. Forum not only helped Hispanic and other veterans, it also got them involved in the civil rights movement. They wanted people from different backgrounds to understand one another. There are still more than 20,000 members of the G.I. Forum today.

Dr. Hector Garcia feels that was his greatest achievement. For his hard work, he received the Presidential Medal of Freedom, the highest honor for an American citizen.

Anthony Quinn (b. 1915)

Lights! Camera! Action! Just think about how fun it would be to act out someone else's life. Actor Anthony Rudolph Oaxaca Quinn was born on April 21, 1915, in Chihuahua, Mexico. His parents were Frank Quinn and Manuella Oaxaca. He became famous after he came to America and became an actor. He became an American citizen in 1947 and has since found many ways to help his community.

At the age of three, Anthony and his mother hid in a coal wagon, crossed the Rio Grande, and ended up in El Paso, Texas. He said he can still remember the taste of coal dust. Yuck! The family left Chihuahua because of the border wars that were going on at that time. A few months later, his father joined his family, and everyone moved to Los Angeles. His father was killed in a serious car accident when Anthony was 13. After that, Anthony worked as a cement mixer, ditch digger, electrician, boxer, and fruit picker to help support his family. When he was 18, he thought about becoming an architect, but didn't think he could afford to go to school for seven years.

Before Anthony got his first job as an actor, he had an operation on his tongue to cure a speech problem. Then in 1935, he was the lead actor in the play *Clean Beds*. That was just the beginning of his acting career. Over the years, he played

Anthony Quinn

many different roles in plays and movies. He was especially good at playing the villain. His hard work as an actor earned him two Oscars from the Academy Awards. He has appeared in dozens of movies since the 1950s.

In 1971, Mr. Quinn was asked by the United States Equal Employment Opportunity Commission (EEOC) to help make a film called *The Voice of La Raza*. This film was about the hard times Puerto Rican and Mexican American people have had in the United States. Since that time, Mr. Quinn has insisted on taking a larger part

in the world, conducting many interviews on racism and children.

Anthony Quinn has been married twice and has nine children. He is a very important person in the Hispanic community.

Dan Sosa (b. 1923)

Think about how hard it would be to be a state Supreme Court judge in New Mexico. That's what Dan Sosa was.

Dan Sosa was born in Las Cruces, New Mexico, in 1923. When he was four years old, his parents got a divorce. After that, he lived with his mom and his sister, Lucy. Young Dan saw how hard his mom was working, and he wanted to help. When he was eight, he started selling newspapers and shining shoes. When he was in high school, he played basketball. His team won the state championship. He was so good that he won a scholarship to New Mexico State University. But soon he had to enter the United States Air Force and fight in World War II.

When he came back from World War II, he used G.I. Bill money from his service in the Air Force to go back to his old school, New Mexico State University. He played basketball, studied to be a teacher, and later became a lawyer. Mr. Sosa worked very hard to become a judge.

Soon, other people found out how smart Judge Sosa was. He was appointed as a justice on the New Mexico Supreme Court. "Money does not make life," Judge Sosa once said. "As a public servant, I make half of what I made before as an attorney.

But real success in life is knowing that you helped others to change their lives for the better."

Judge Dan Sosa worked for many years on the New Mexico Supreme Court. He is trying to change the laws so that everyone can get a job regardless of the color of their skin. He believes people should work hard and try to improve their lives. Judge Sosa and his wife have three daughters and 17 grandchildren.

Julian Nava (b. 1927)

Julian Nava was the first Mexican American on the Los Angeles Board of Education in this century.

When Julian was young, his father owned a barber shop. Julian listened to people talk about the government. "When I was growing up," he said, "I thought Anglos were smarter than Mexicans."

After high school, Julian joined the Navy and learned that it was the job a person did that mattered, not the color of their skin or their background. He decided to study history. He was student body president at East Los Angeles Junior College. He later went to Pomona College and Harvard University to earn his doctorate. He was very proud because it is difficult to get this degree.

When he was teaching history at San Fernando Valley State College, Dr. Nava wanted to write the story of Mexican Americans. "Mexican Americans are identified as losers in almost all works of history that deal with them," he said. He wanted to change that. His book was entitled *Mexican Americans:*

Past, Present and Future. He also wrote a reading series for schools about Mexican Americans that is written in both English and Spanish.

In 1967, Dr. Nava ran for a position on the Board of Education of Los Angeles. He got help from people all over the city and became the first Mexican American to win that job. Later, he became president of the school board. Dr. Julian Nava is an

Bishop Patrick Flores

important historian and leader. He's also a great role model.

Patrick Flores (b. 1929)

Patrick Flores was the smartest kid in his high school. When he was 20, he entered the seminary. This is a special school for men who are studying to be priests.

Patrick became a priest in 1956. He was a very popular priest. When he said Mass, he sometimes used mariachi music. At the time he was ordained, there were only two Hispanic priests in the Houston area of Texas.

Bishop Flores has helped many people. Once, he raffled off his gold bishop's ring to help an innocent man who had been thrown in prison. Bishop Flores raised enough money for the man's lawyer, and the bishop's ring was returned to him because he was so kind.

Bishop Flores raises money for a battered women's shelter and has a telethon that benefits the homeless, the needy, the elderly, and the ill. The telethon helps pay emergency rent and utilities, and buys medication for these people.

Although the job of a bishop is very serious, Bishop Flores is willing to participate in silly events for good causes. He participated in the "Kiss-a-Pig" contest for the American Diabetes Foundation. In this contest, the person who raises the most money is given the privilege of "kissing a pig" to thank it for its by-products used to make insulin—the medicine used by people with diabetes.

On October 13, 1979, Patrick Flores became Archbishop of San Antonio, Texas. Bishop Flores has spent his whole life helping others.

Jaime Escalante (b. 1931)

Have you ever seen the movie *Stand and Deliver*? This movie tells the story of a math teacher named Jaime Escalante. Mr. Escalante was such a good teacher that 80 percent of his math students passed an advanced placement test for college credit. In our whole country, only two out of every 100 seniors take this advanced placement test.

Jaime Escalante is known as one of the best teachers in the United States. He was born in the country of Bolivia. In Bolivia, he taught a very difficult type of math called calculus. He left Bolivia because the government was fighting and he didn't feel safe. He came to America with his wife, Fabiola, and his son, Jaime Jr.

When he came to the United States, he didn't teach right away, because he couldn't speak English, and he didn't have the right degree to teach here. So he worked in a coffee shop and taught himself English. Later, he got a job with a company, but didn't like it. Then he went to college at night for seven years to get his math degree. Afterward, he found a job teaching math at Garfield High School.

One time, the people who graded tests told him that some of his students must be cheating on the advanced placement test, because they had a lot of the same mistakes. They all had to take the test again to find out if anyone had cheated. Every one of the students proved they didn't cheat by passing the test again.

Mr. Escalante is such a good math teacher that he never stops teaching. He even helps his students study on Saturdays. He likes to work with his students and won't accept less than their best. He often begins his classes with a cheerleading song about math. By being such an inspiring teacher, Jaime Escalante helps his students work hard and believe in themselves.

Rita Moreno (b. 1931)

Rita Moreno was born on December 11, 1931, in Humacao, Puerto Rico. Humacao

Rita Moreno

is near a rain forest. The name she was given when she was born was Rosa Dolores Alverio. In 1950, she decided to change her name to Rita Moreno. Rita was for her first name, Rosita, and Moreno was the last name of her stepfather.

When Rita Moreno was five years old, she traveled on a ship to New York. She was so poor that she had to live in the slums. She had a hard time at school because she only spoke Spanish. It was difficult to find people who could speak Spanish and teach her English. Ms. Moreno dropped out of school when she was 16 and started taking singing and dancing lessons.

After a lot of hard work, she won an Academy Award in 1952 for acting in the movie *West Side Story*. This made her famous all around the world. She also won a Tony Award for playing Googie Gomez in a play called *The Ritz*. Rita Moreno received two Emmy Awards for other acting she did on TV. She also won a musical award called a Grammy for an album she recorded.

Rita Moreno is a great hero because she is the first woman in the world to win all four of the highest awards in show business.

Roberto Clemente (1934–1972)

Roberto Clemente was one of the best baseball players that ever lived, but he was forced to play in the minor leagues because of the color of his skin. Even though this happened to him, Mr. Clemente went on to have a great career.

Roberto Clemente was born in Carolina, Puerto Rico, on August 18, 1934. He was

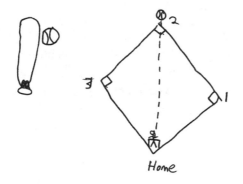

Home

small as a boy, and his family was very poor. He made his own baseballs out of old golf balls wrapped with tape. By the time he was in high school, he was a great baseball player. The Los Angeles Dodgers drafted him when he was 18 to play professional baseball. The Dodgers' scout in Puerto Rico, Al Campanis, said Roberto Clemente was the greatest natural athlete he had ever seen.

The Dodgers were afraid that their fans would not like the idea of three players who were not white playing in the same outfield. So they put Mr. Clemente in the minor leagues, which was hard for him. "I want to go home," he said. "I am not being used!" He knew he was better than the other players.

But then Mr. Clemente was drafted by the Pittsburgh Pirates. When the people in Pittsburgh saw him play, they knew he was special. Mr. Clemente became one of the very best baseball players ever. In his dozen or so years playing baseball, he won four batting championships and led the Pirates to two World Series victories. He finished his career with 3,000 hits.

In 1972, there was a terrible earthquake in Nicaragua. Many people were killed or left homeless. Mr. Clemente helped collect food, supplies, and medicine. He flew on a plane to take these things to Nicaragua. On the way, the plane crashed into the ocean, and his body was never found. His family and fans were heartbroken. Mr. Clemente was only 37 when he died.

Three months later, Roberto Clemente was elected into the Baseball Hall of Fame. His wife, Vera, and his three sons went to the ceremony. Later, one of his sons started a program to bring baseball to inner-city kids in Pittsburgh. Today, Roberto Clemente is still remembered as a great baseball player and a kind man who helped others.

Katherine Ortega (b. 1934)

In 1983, Katherine Davalos Ortega was nominated to be America's 38th treasurer. She was the tenth woman to have this important and powerful position.

The Ortega family owned and ran a restaurant and dance hall in a small town in New Mexico. The Ortega children received a good education from their father. He believed that if you had a strong education, you would be able to care for yourself and to help others. Katherine went to school regularly, learned English, and received awards for perfect attendance. She loved math and working with money, so she worked as a waitress and cashier in her family's restaurant. Her dad used to depend on her to keep track of how much money he made.

In the late 1950s, Ms. Ortega graduated with honors from Eastern New Mexico

University with a degree in business and economics. She also learned how to teach high school. She became locally famous because she was the first woman president of a bank in California. In 1982, President Ronald Reagan appointed Ms. Ortega to be on an advisory committee on small and minority business.

After that, she became the United States treasurer. Ms. Ortega worked hard to do her job. Part of her job was to sign her name on the money that people spend. If you look at a dollar bill today, you might find Katherine Ortega's signature on it. She isn't the treasurer anymore, but is still working hard to help other people learn about money.

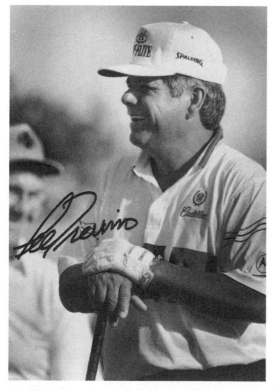

Lee Trevino

Lee Trevino (b. 1939)

Lee Trevino is a champion in golf. Everyone cheers for him and they call him "Super Mex" when he makes a great shot. Mr. Trevino has worked hard to be a champion.

Lee Trevino and his sister grew up with their mother and grandfather in Dallas, Texas. When Mr. Trevino was six years old, he found a left-handed golf club in a hayfield. He was right-handed, but he kept the club anyway. He dug holes in the hayfield and made his own golf course. He practiced and practiced all the time. His hard work paid off because he became a good player.

In 1967, when Mr. Trevino was accepted as a member of the Professional Golf Association (PGA), he was very happy. He was so good that he was honored as the "Sportsman of the Year" by *Sports Illustrated* in 1971. He has also been honored for helping others. He says he likes all people, and he doesn't care what color skin people have. Mr. Trevino gives money to charities and helps the poor and sick people. Lee Trevino is a true Mexican American hero.

Vikki Carr (b. 1940)

Did you know that Vikki Carr is a famous singer? She performs in the best nightclubs. She is one of the world's best-selling singers.

She was born in El Paso, Texas, as Florencia Bisenta de Casillas Martinez Cardona and grew up in Rosemead, California. She is the oldest of seven children. Vikki first sang in public at the age of four. In high school, she took lots of music classes and sang in musical plays. She was also in a

Mexican-Irish band. Her first hit song for Liberty Records was "It Must Be Him." Later, she sang in both English and Spanish. One song that she performed was called *"Cuando Caliente el Sol."*

Growing up, Vikki spoke Spanish and English, but nobody knew she was Hispanic because of her light skin. She is very proud of her Mexican heritage. She helped save Holy Cross High School in San Antonio, Texas, from being closed. It was located in a poor section of the city. She raised more than $50,000 to save the school. The students gave Ms. Carr a bracelet for her efforts.

Ms. Carr has performed at the White House for former Presidents Nixon and Ford. She raised money for scholarships to help more students go to college. Her favorite song says, "I can only give you love that lasts forever." That's how Vikki Carr feels about life.

Martin Sheen

Martin Sheen (b. 1940)

Martin Sheen has been an actor in a lot of hit movies. Now his kids are doing the same thing. Mr. Sheen's kids are Emilio Estevez, Charlie Sheen, Ramon Sheen, and Renee Estevez. Mr. Sheen is proud of all of his children.

Ramon Estevez, who later changed his name to Martin Sheen, was born August 3, 1940. He has nine brothers and sisters. His mother died when he was only 11. He went to Catholic schools, where he decided that he really wanted to be an actor. When he was a senior in high school, Martin Sheen won first place in a talent show and won a free trip to New York. He decided to drop out of high school and move to New York. He took any job that was close to actors. He even served as a janitor for an off-Broadway theater. He changed his name to Martin Sheen so that he wouldn't get only Hispanic acting parts. He got Martin from Robert Dale Martin, a CBS casting director, and Sheen from Bishop Fulton J. Sheen.

It was hard finding acting work, but finally he got work acting in plays. A few years later, he starred on TV shows like *The Defenders* and *East Side, West Side*. Then he started to make a lot of movies. His best movies were *Badlands, Gandhi, Wall Street*, and *Apocalypse Now*. Mr. Sheen had a near-fatal heart attack when he was filming *Apocalypse Now* in the Philippines. He was alone and had to drag himself to help.

Now Mr. Sheen is an activist and an actor, and demonstrates for causes that he believes in. During good and bad times, Martin Sheen has always worked to help others. He likes to tell others about his Catholic religion and tries to make the world better for his grandchildren. Mr. Sheen lives with his wife, Janet, in Malibu, California. They have been married 34 years.

Joan Baez (b. 1941)

It would be hard to convince people all over the world to make peace with one another.

Joan Baez tries to do this. "My concern has always been for the people who are victimized, unable to speak for themselves, and who need help," the singer once said.

Joan Baez was born on Staten Island, New York. She was one of the three daughters of Joan Bridge and Alberto Baez. Her father was a scientist and a former physicist and university professor. Her family moved to California when she was little. Joan felt alone and different because she was part Scottish and part Mexican. She started getting into singing groups in junior high school. She made some more friends by dancing in high school. Ms. Baez started college, but didn't like it. One night her dad took her to a coffeehouse where young people were showing off their talents. She fit right in. She started working as a singer and guitar player. Her music helped many Americans understand their feelings about peace, war, and injustice.

Ms. Baez dreamed of having her own family. The first time she met her husband was at a dance in New York City. He looked at her and winked. From that first meeting, their love blossomed. They got married a year later. After a while, three daughters were born. Joan Baez still lives in New York with her husband and kids. She is still working to educate and entertain her audiences.

Ritchie Valens (1941–1959)

As a boy, Richard Valenzuela lived with his mom and sisters. When he was 12 years old, he bought a guitar. He loved his guitar and practiced a lot in his garage. All of his life, he only had one dream—to sing. He didn't ignore his dream.

When Ritchie was 17, he started singing in public. A music producer watched him sing. The producer decided young Ritchie had talent, and he gave him his first record contract. He was told that if he wanted to make it big, he would have to change his name so it didn't sound so Hispanic. He shortened his name to Ritchie Valens. At his first real concert, he played and sang as though his life depended on it. Everything was going well for him.

Ritchie Valens wrote almost every song he sang, except for the famous song, *La Bamba*. Ritchie wrote *Come On, Let's Go* and *Donna*, a song for his girlfriend.

On February 4, 1959, on a stormy, snowy night after a concert in Clear Lake, Iowa, Ritchie, Buddy Holly, and the Big Bopper got on a charter plane to go home. They never made it. Three of America's favorite rock stars were killed when the plane crashed in a cornfield. Ritchie was only 17 years old.

In 1988, a movie of Ritchie's life, *La Bamba*, was released. It was a huge hit. It was written and directed by Luis Valdez. Los Lobos, a Hispanic rock band, recorded the music. Thirty years after the songs were written, a new generation of rock music lovers discovered the music of Ritchie Valens.

Vilma Martinez (b. 1943)

Vilma Martinez is an important person because she is president of the Mexican American Legal Defense and Educational Fund (MALDEF), an organization that helps

Vilma Martinez

others. She is also chairperson of the University of California Board of Regents.

Vilma Martinez was born on October 17, 1943, in San Antonio, Texas. She went to school there, and one of her teachers wanted her to go to a technical high school, where she would learn how to do work. Vilma didn't want to do that—she wanted to go to a high school where she would be able to take classes that would get her ready for college. So she went to school, did all of her homework, and became very educated. In 1967, she graduated from Columbia University Law School and became a lawyer.

In 1973, Ms. Martinez was made president of MALDEF. MALDEF helps Mexican Americans have their own place to live, and makes sure that good things happen for them. She worked hard in 1974 for bilingual education—the right for Hispanic students to be taught in both English and Spanish. Vilma Martinez still struggles for the rights of other people. Her whole job has been to work against discrimination.

Antonia Novello (b. 1944)

Imagine being the very first woman and the very first Hispanic Surgeon General of the United States. The Surgeon General is the person who helps take care of America's health, by warning people of things that

Antonia Novello

could hurt them and letting them know about things that are good for them, too.

Antonia Novello was born on August 23, 1944, in Fajardo, Puerto Rico. She lived with her parents, her brother, and her sister. Even though she was born with intestinal problems that caused her lots of pain for many years, Antonia played softball and was president of her class in school.

When Ms. Novello was 18, she had to see a doctor at a special clinic in Minnesota. To pay for her doctor bills, she took care of her doctor's kids and taught them Spanish. She decided to become a doctor so she could help other children.

After Ms. Novello got better, she went to the University of Puerto Rico in San Juan and got a bachelor's degree in biology. Then she went to medical school at the University of Puerto Rico. In 1970, she was finally a real medical doctor! After that, Dr. Novello went to the University of Michigan to study more about children and to learn how to take care of them. In 1982, she got a master's degree in public health from Johns Hopkins University in Baltimore, Maryland. From 1986 to 1990, Dr. Novello worked at the National Institute of Health. At the end of the year, she was made deputy director of the National Institute of Child Health and Human Development.

In March of 1990, Dr. Novello became the 14th Surgeon General. Today, she warns people about AIDS, diet and health, the dangers of smoking, and environmental health hazards. We are very proud of Dr. Antonia Novello because she has one of the most important jobs in America.

Jose Feliciano (b. 1945)

What would you do if you wanted to learn to play the guitar, but couldn't see it? Jose Feliciano is blind and learned to play a guitar. He also, sings, writes music, and plays a lot of other instruments.

Jose Feliciano was born September 22, 1945, in Lares, Puerto Rico. He is the second of 11 boys. The Felicianos moved from Puerto Rico to New York when Jose was very young.

Jose couldn't play sports because he was blind, but he could play the accordion when he was just six years old, and the guitar by the time he was nine! He was inspired by Elvis Presley, Ray Charles, Sam Cooke, Otis Redding, Fats Domino, and Chuck Berry. He hoped he could be just like them someday.

He played at local events, talent shows, and assemblies. When he was 17, he dropped out of high school to help his family. A record company signed him later that year.

In 1964, he appeared at the Newport Jazz Festival. He sang a lot of Spanish songs. In 1968, he became popular singing English songs. One example was "Light My Fire"— a song made popular by the Doors—but Jose sang it in his own style. Later that year, he sang the "Star-Spangled Banner" at the World Series. He is most famous for singing "Feliz Navidad." Listen carefully, you will probably hear "Feliz Navidad" on the radio during Christmas time.

Mr. Feliciano has performed with many symphonies. In 1991, he became a disc jockey. Then he married Susan, and now they have a daughter and a son. Jose Feliciano even had the pleasure of playing for Pope John Paul II. His dream of becoming a famous performer had come true beyond his wildest expectations!

Edward James Olmos (center) portrayed Jamie Escalante in the movie Stand and Deliver. *Here, he poses with some of the authors.*

Linda Ronstadt (b. 1946)

Linda Ronstadt was born July 15, 1946, and raised in Tucson, Arizona. Her father sang Mexican music on local radio stations and did shows with big bands. She and her four siblings all liked their dad's music. They enjoyed listening to his records at family gatherings and during trips they took to Mexico to visit relatives.

When Ms. Ronstadt was 18, she left Tucson to go to Los Angeles. After lots of hard work, she became a rock star. She doesn't speak Spanish well, but she loves Mexican music, and hasn't forgotten about her heritage. Ms. Ronstadt has recorded about 50 albums, and 15 of them have been bestsellers. She sings in English on most of her albums, but two of her Spanish albums

are *Canciónes de mi Padre* ("Songs of My Father") and *Más Canciónes de mi Padre* ("More Songs of My Father"). We were surprised to learn that, even though she is a big star, Linda Ronstadt still has stage fright!

Edward James Olmos (b. 1947)

Edward James Olmos is famous because he is an actor, singer, dancer, director, and musician. He has worked in theaters, movies, and television.

Edward James Olmos was born on February 24, 1947, in California. He has one older brother and one younger sister. In the 1950s, his parents got divorced. Edward worked hard in school because a good education was very important to him. He went to California State University during the day and played in his band at night, because he had to have money to pay for school. When the band took a break, Edward would study very hard.

Edward was also a fantastic actor. He took theater and dance classes. By the early 1970s, Edward was acting in TV shows. He worked in plays and acted in a movie about the zoot-suit riots. He was a police lieutenant on *Miami Vice* and played Jaime Escalante in the movie *Stand and Deliver*.

Edward James Olmos is a great helper. He gives speeches during tours, does charity work, and spends time with his family. He even helped clean up after the Los Angeles earthquake in 1994. He is a great example of the talent and determination found in the Mexican American culture.

Federico Pena

Federico Pena (b. 1947)

Federico Pena was elected mayor of Denver, Colorado, when he was 36 years old. He was very proud because he was one of the youngest mayors of a big city in the United States.

Federico Pena was born on March 15, 1947, in Laredo, Texas. He is the third child of six kids. He was a very busy child. He played 11 sports in high school! When Federico was growing up, his parents wanted to be sure that he went to school. They were strict, and the children in the family had to call them "sir" and "ma'am." His parents believed that everybody should go to school, so all six of the Pena children did. They all have college degrees, too.

Before he became mayor of Denver, he worked hard to become a lawyer. He worked with the Chicano Education Project and the Mexican American Legal Defense Fund. He was elected to the Colorado House of Representatives. In 1983, the people of Denver voted for him to be their mayor. He told people to "imagine a great city." While he was mayor, Federico Pena worked on problems of air pollution, building a new airport, raising money to run the city, and building a convention center where businesspeople could meet. He also helped to get a new mall built.

Mayor Pena went to the people who were in charge of major league baseball and asked them if Denver could have a baseball team.

They said yes! That is how the Colorado Rockies got started. After being mayor for eight years, he started his own investment company called Pena Investment Advisors, Inc. In 1992, Bill Clinton became President of the United States and needed someone to be secretary of transportation. Federico Pena wanted this job and got it, so he packed up his family and all of their things and moved to Washington, D.C.

Secretary Pena is a person who doesn't quit and is working hard to make things better for his family and all the people in the United States.

Jim Plunkett (b. 1947)

A lot of people saw the amazing things that Jim Plunkett did on the football field, but his parents saw nothing because they were both blind. Jim Plunkett was born on December 5, 1947, in San Jose, California. His mother, Carmen, is Mexican, and his father, William, is Irish. Jim's life as a young boy was very hard. He worked many hours to help support his family. He mowed lawns, gardened, and even delivered newspapers. He learned about hard work from his parents. "I got a lot of support from my parents," says Jim Plunkett. "It wasn't until later that I noticed having blind parents was unusual."

Jim went to Mayfair Elementary School. He had good grades in school. At recess, his favorite sport was football. He played lots of football. Jim became a better player because he practiced and worked hard. He led his team to the county championship. He earned a scholarship to Stanford University and in 1970 he won college football's highest honor, the Heisman Trophy. As the country's best quarterback, he led his team to win the Rose Bowl.

Jim Plunkett was the first player drafted into the NFL in 1970. He did such a good job as the quarterback for the New England Patriots that he was named Rookie of the Year. Unfortunately, he kept getting sacked. Over the next few years, he had surgery several times, and he lost a lot of confidence. He ended up spending two rocky seasons sitting on the bench for the San Francisco 49ers. When the 49ers finally cut him from the team, he thought his football career was over. Then the Oakland Raiders ask him to play, and in 1981 he took them to the Super Bowl. They won, and Mr. Plunkett was chosen as the Most Valuable Player.

Mr. Plunkett believes that if kids play sports, they will stay out of trouble. Some kids don't have money to buy the expensive equipment, so Mr. Plunkett has tried to get it for them. He has worked hard to make sure that teams for young people have the athletic equipment they need. Now that Jim Plunkett is retired from football, he has even more time to work with Mexican American girls and boys. He is a role model for all kids.

Jimmy Smits (b. 1956)

Jimmy Smits was born in 1956 and raised in the tough city of Brooklyn, New York. His mom was from Puerto Rico and his dad was from a country on the northeastern coast of South America called Suriname. The people there come from many different cultures.

His father was the manager of a factory that made film used for silk screening, and his mom was a nurse's aide. He has two younger sisters. Yvonne is now a nurse, and Dianna is a secretary on Wall Street in New York.

When Jimmy was a boy, he always liked making an audience laugh at his impressions of Ed Sullivan. Then when he was 18, his parents got divorced and he became the man of the house.

Mr. Smits has a daughter named Taina and a son named Joaquin. When his kids were little, Mr. Smits graduated from Brooklyn College and received a master's degree from Cornell University.

Mr. Smits' parents wanted him to be a teacher because they wanted him to have a secure job. But Mr. Smits decided he would follow his heart and go into acting. He made it big on a TV show called *L.A. Law*. Since then, he's also made some movies. Now he's back on TV doing a show called *N.Y.P.D. Blues*. Mr. Smits likes this because now he is closer to his family in New York.

Someday Mr. Smits wants to act in plays. He likes plays by William Shakespeare, Federico Garcia Lorca, and Pedro Calderon de la Barca. But most of all, he wants to act in a play by Anton Chekov, who is Mr. Smits' favorite playwright.

As an actor, Jimmy Smits' goal is to show that Hispanics can be smart, successful, and just as good as everyone else.

Gloria Estefan (b. 1957)

Gloria Maria Fajardo was born September 1, 1957, in Havana, Cuba. Her father was a motorcycle policeman and a bodyguard for President Batista. Her mom was a teacher and translator. Her sister, Becky, is five years younger than she is. When Gloria was only 14 months old, her family fled Cuba with few belongings when Fidel Castro rose to power. They moved to Miami, Florida. She had a poor childhood.

Gloria started singing when she was three years old. If she wanted to cry, she would go in her room and sing instead. Gloria grew up and joined a band that played on weekends. She married Emilio Estefan in 1978, and their group, Miami Sound Machine, became a big hit. Their music can be heard in such movies as *Top Gun* and *Three Men and a Baby*.

In 1991, the bus that Gloria Estefan was on was suddenly rear-ended by two other buses. When she realized that she couldn't move from the waist down, she was really scared. She was worried that she wouldn't be able to walk, dance, or sing ever again. Ms. Estefan showed lots of courage and determination to live through the accident. She wanted to tell about the difficult recovery from her broken back, so she sang a song called "Into the Light."

Gloria Estefan is a very successful singer, composer, and dancer. Her husband, Emilio, is a producer, songwriter, and agent. Gloria and Emilio have two children, Nayib and Emily. Emily was born after Gloria's near-fatal bus accident.

Nancy Lopez (b. 1957)

If you know golf, you know Nancy Lopez. Ms. Lopez has become a famous golfer because she is talented and works very hard. She was born on January 6, 1957, in Torrance, California. When she was only nine years old, she won a pee-wee golf tournament. When she was 12, she played in three state tournaments and won one of them. She was on her way!

Nancy had to work very hard because her coach was her father. He was also tough on her when she did her chores at home. But guess what? Nancy didn't have to do the dishes, because they would make her hands soft, which would be bad for her golf game.

When Nancy Lopez was 19, she became a professional golfer. She won five major tournaments in a row! She is the youngest woman ever to be elected into the Ladies' Professional Golf Association (LPGA) Hall of Fame. Her goal when she golfs is to keep breaking her own records. She feels she is a role model for Hispanic people and tries always to be honest. In ten years, Nancy Lopez has won 39 tournaments and more than $2 million! She also takes time to sign autographs, give interviews, pose for pictures, and shake hands. She volunteers for "Aid for the Handicapped," which helps kids who are blind or deaf. Ms. Lopez married Ray Knight in 1986. They have two girls, Erin and Ashley. She is proud to be a mother and wife. Her family is so important that when she is at home in Florida, Nancy focuses on her family instead of golf.

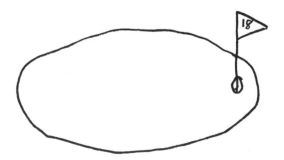

even raise her hand in school. She was too embarrassed to answer questions.

Evelyn's mom decided to put her in ballet classes so that maybe she wouldn't be so shy. At first she was very shy, but she got better and people liked the way she danced, so she wasn't so shy any more. Even though her family could only afford to send her to ballet class once a week, she made sure that she practiced every day.

Ms. Cisneros got so good at dancing that she won awards and a medal. She performed in the play *Romeo and Juliet* and in the ballet *Sleeping Beauty*. The people in the audience said she was as pretty as Sleeping Beauty. She has danced at the White House, and was a main ballerina for the San Francisco Ballet Company.

Nancy Lopez hopes people will remember her as a nice person and as one of the best woman golfers.

Evelyn Cisneros (b. 1958)

Evelyn Cisneros was born in California on November 18, 1958. When she was young, she was different from most other California kids around her because she had dark skin and black hair. Being the only Mexican made Evelyn very shy. When she was seven years old, she was so shy that she didn't

Ellen Ochoa

Evelyn Cisneros is married and has two cats. She also has a brother named Robert, who was a very good tap dancer.

Ellen Ochoa (b. 1959)

Try to imagine how it would feel if you were an astronaut for the space shuttle program of the National Aeronautics and Space Administration (NASA). Ellen Ochoa achieved that goal. She became the first Hispanic woman astronaut. She wanted young Hispanic girls to look up to her as one of their role models.

Ellen Ochoa was born in San Diego, California, in 1959. Her parents got divorced when she was in junior high. She grew up with her mother, three brothers, and one sister in La Mesa, California. When she was very young, her mother taught her that getting an education was important. She went to school at San Diego State University. She studied hard and got a degree in electrical engineering.

Ms. Ochoa always wanted to be an astronaut, but she didn't know if she could do it. After getting her pilot's license and starting graduate school, she realized she had the qualifications to become an astronaut. In 1990, she became NASA's first Hispanic woman astronaut.

Ms. Ochoa's message to all people who want to reach their goals is, "If you stay in school, you have the potential to achieve what you want in the future." She believes that kids should stay in school because "education increases career options and gives you a chance for a wide variety of jobs."

Since Ms. Ochoa doesn't have children, she likes it when kids come to NASA for tours. Ellen Ochoa loves her job because it is exciting. She plans to keep it her whole life.

Fernando Valenzuela (b. 1960)

Imagine being the youngest baseball player in history and still helping your team win the championship. Well, that's what Fernando Valenzuela did.

Fernando Valenzuela was born on November 1, 1960, in a tiny village of Etchohuaquila in northern Mexico. His parents are Avelino and Emerjilda. Fernando is the youngest of 12 children. He went to public schools in Mexico, but sometimes played baseball instead of going to school. He played for his village's home team and for the Sonora state team.

When he was just 15, Fernando was signed on as a professional baseball player in Mexico. He was scouted by Mike Brito from the Los Angeles Dodgers in 1979. Mr. Brito was very impressed with his abilities and asked him if he'd like to play baseball in America. So Fernando moved to Los Angeles, played for a couple of farm teams, and learned how to throw a screwball before he was offered a contract to play in the major leagues. He became the youngest player in baseball history when he signed that contract with the Dodgers.

As a left-handed pitcher, Mr. Valenzuela was called the king of screwballs. The screwball is one of the hardest baseball pitches to throw. When the season began, all of the starting pitchers were hurt, so Mr.

Valenzuela got to start the game. During that season, he helped the Dodgers tie the Houston Astros for the West Division championship. Fernando Valenzuela was named the National League Rookie of the Year. He also won the Cy Young Award, which is given to the best pitcher in the National League. A rookie has never won this award before.

Tony Melendez (b. 1963)

Tony Melendez has never let anything stop him just because he doesn't have arms. He has been on the *Geraldo Show* and the *Oprah Winfrey Show*, and has performed seven concerts with Linda Ronstadt.

Tony Melendez was born in 1963 in Nicaragua. Before he was born, his mom took a pill that her doctor gave her to make her feel better. The pill was called Thalidomide. Doctors found out later that these pills hurt babies before they were born. That is why Tony was born without any arms.

Tony's family came to the United States when he was just a baby. When he was little, Tony used his toes to build with blocks and to color pictures. He also liked to sing songs. When he was 16, he brought home an old guitar and started playing it with his toes! Two months later, he could play "Mary Had a Little Lamb" and "Home on the Range"! He practiced every day and became a very good guitar player and singer. Soon he started giving concerts across the country. Mr. Melendez tells kids that they should reach out and grab their dreams.

Mr. Melendez has a really neat family. His parents had seven kids and decided there was still room for more. So they adopted four kids, for a total of 13 people in the Melendez family. Mr. Melendez has learned a lot from his family. His father always said, "Nobody is unadoptable. All they need is a lot of love and attention from their brothers and sisters." In 1986, the Melendez family was America's Hispanic Family of the Year, and they were also considered one of six Great American Families by the American Family Society. They won a trip to the White House because of these awards and got to meet former First Lady Nancy Reagan.

Once Mr. Melendez had a chance to play for Pope John Paul II when the Pope was visiting the United States. From that day on, his whole life changed. He has signed a contract for a movie and has written a book about his life. He has made record albums in Spanish and English. He has spread an important message, singing in countries

around the world. Tony Melendez is bringing the gift of hope to all people.

Michael Carbajal (b. 1968)

Have you ever dreamed of becoming a world-champion boxer or an Olympic medalist? Michael Carbajal reached both of those goals.

Michael Carbajal was born in 1968 in Arizona. But the Carbajal family had lived in Arizona for a long time already. Their relatives had moved there from Mexico during the late 1800s, before Arizona had even become a state.

Michael's father, Manuel, was the Arizona Golden Gloves Flyweight Champion in the late 1940s. Manuel taught all nine of his children to box—even his three girls. Of all his brothers and sisters, Michael was the one to achieve greatness in boxing.

Michael worked out in the backyard boxing ring that Danny, his brother and trainer, had built for him. Michael's first boxing award came from the 1981 Southwest Optimist Tournament. Later, he won a silver medal in the 1988 Summer Olympics in Seoul, Korea. He calls himself

"manitos de piedra" which means "little hands of stone."

In 1990, Michael Carbajal became the International Boxing Federation Junior Flyweight World Champion. He also signed a three-year contract with the NBC television network to show his fights on TV.

Giselle Fernandez (b. 1971)

Did you know that Giselle Fernandez is a newscaster? She was born in Mexico, went to college in California, and then got a job as a news reporter. She has done lots of things for her job, like doing research, interviewing interesting people, and writing the stories that are read on the news. She has traveled to Somalia, Israel, Cuba, London, California, and Panama. She has been a reporter in Chicago, Miami, Los Angeles, and Colorado Springs. Sometimes she substitutes for anchorman Dan Rather on the CBS Evening News.

Ms. Fernandez is single. She enjoys dancing, running, and reading. Giselle Fernandez likes her job very much and

enjoys being on TV. We all know that she is an important role model for children, because she has worked to make her dreams come true.

Selena (1971–1995)

Selena was a brilliant star who died tragically at a very young age. She was a singer who was very well known here in the United States, and in Mexico and other Latin American countries.

Selena Quintanilla was born in Lake Jackson, Texas, on April 16, 1971. When she was nine, she started out with the group Selena y los Dinos. Her brother and sister were part of the group when they recorded their first album. Later Selena went solo, but kept her band. Her father, Abrahm Quintanilla, was her agent.

When she was 18, Selena married Chris Perez, the guitarist of Selena y los Dinos. If she had lived, Selena probably would have had children because she wanted to be a mother. She won a Grammy for her album *Selena Live* and she appeared in *Don Juan de Marco*, a movie that was released after she died. Selena also started two of her own clothing stores in Texas with some of her own clothing designs. The stores were called Selena's Etc. One was in Corpus Christi, and the other was in San Antonio.

On March 31, 1995, Selena's life came to a tragic end. Selena went to a motel to meet Yolanda Saldivar, who used to be her fan-club organizer and manager of Selena's stores. Selena went to pick up some papers, they had an argument, and Yolanda shot Selena in the shoulder and back. She died in the operating room that same day. Yolanda Saldivar was charged with her murder and sentenced to life in prison.

Selena was working on her first English language CD right before she died. Since her death, her album, *Dreaming of You*, has done well, selling 350,000 copies in its first week. Selena is still admired and missed by her fans. She achieved in death what she wished for in life.

MORE FAMOUS FIRSTS AND HEROES

The list of Hispanic people who have accomplished great things could go on and on. Look for some of the following names in newspapers, magazines, and books. The library is a great place to find out more.

Anaya, Rudolfo A.
Novelist. Wrote several books including *Bless Me, Ultima*.

Anguiano, Lupe
A Roman Catholic nun, teacher, and social activist.

Aragon, Manuel Jr.
Mayor of Los Angeles, California.

Arnaz, Desi
Famous Cuban entertainer, married Lucille Ball.

Baez, Albert
Physicist, environmentalist who worked with UNICEF.

Blades, Ruben
Lawyer, singer, actor. Won four Grammy Awards and gold records. Acted in *The Milagro Beanfield War.*

Castro, Raul
Governor of Arizona in 1975. Judge of juvenile court.

Cisneros, Henry
First Mexican American mayor of San Antonio, Texas. Secretary of HUD (Housing and Urban Development).

Codina, Armando M.
Miami's most influential business and political leader. Director of three *Fortune 100* companies.

Collazo, Francisco J.
President, CEO of largest Hispanic-owned engineering firm in nation (Colsa Corporation).

de la Renta, Oscar
Successful fashion designer.

del Campo, Martin
Architect, patriot. Once said, "Mexican culture is a combination of smells and sounds."

Senator Henry Gonzalez

Delgado, Abelardo
Famous Chicano poet, wrote about social reform and the feminist movement. Author of 14 books.

Feldenkreis, George and Family
Started "Supreme International," producer of men's and boys' clothing.

Fernandez, Mary Jo
First to win all four age divisions in the Rolex Orange Bowl World Junior Championships.

Fuentes, Tito
Famous for playing the congos. Part of the Mambo Kings.

Galarza, Ernesto
Writer and scholar, devoted to bilingual education.

Gonzalez, Henry B.
First Hispanic senator of Texas. Helped get benefits for Hispanic Vietnam War veterans.

Gutierrez, Jose Angel
Worked for PASO, the Political Association of Spanish-speaking Organizations. Founded La Raza Unida.

Hayworth, Rita
Legendary motion-picture star, danced with Fred Astaire.

Hernandez, Enrigue Sr.
Retired police officer. Started Intercon Security Systems in California.

Jaramillo, Mari-Luci
Educator, teacher-trainer for bilingual education.

Lapciuc, Israel
Businessman, owns Precision Trading Corporation, an electronics firm.

Liberman, Elias, Jose, and Julio
Bought and sold Spanish language stations in Southern California.

Lopez, George A. and Family
Physician, invented Click Lock, special device to secure hypodermic needles into intravenous lines.

Melantzon, Ricardo Aquilar
Writer, poet, professor at University of Texas, El Paso.

Montalban, Ricardo
Famous actor in Hollywood. Star of the movie *Star Trek II*

Montoya, Joseph
Youngest man ever elected to New Mexico state legislature.

Nicolas, Emilio Sr. and Family
Founder of Spanish International Network (SIN).

Olivarez, Grace Gil
First woman to graduate from Notre Dame University.

Paredes, Americo
Teacher, musician, scholar, and collector of folk songs.

Pele (Edson Anontes do Nascimento)
Brazilian soccer player, responsible for bringing soccer to U.S. Scored 1,200 goals in 1,253 games. Considered the greatest soccer player of his time.

Rivera, Geraldo
Famous TV journalist, has own talk show. Law degree from the University of Pennsylvania, degree in journalism from Columbia University. Received Peabody Award, ten Emmys for important broadcast journalism.

Rodriguez, Johnny
Received Grammy from Academy of Country-Western Music as "Most Promising Vocalist."

Rodriguez, Juan "Chi Chi"
Golfer, won eight PGA Tours. Known as "Clown Prince of the Tour" for entertaining crowds.

Romero, Cesar
Famous actor. The Joker in *Batman* television series.

Roybal, Edward R.
Member of United States House of Representatives. Helped write Bilingual Education Act.

Sabates, Felix
Owns minor league hockey team, Charlotte Checkers, and has a NASCAR auto racing team.

Santana, Carlos
Real name: Autlan de Novarra. Permanent influence on rock music scene. In 1969 formed blues band playing a mixture of Afro-Cuban rhythm with a mellow kind of rock.

Sepulveda, Frank Sr. and Family
Built wealth from selling produce. Recently sold their 21-store chain of Handy Andy supermarkets.

Torres, Arturo G.
Operates Tex-Mex restaurants in Spain. Owns Play by Play Toys and Novelties.

Unanue, Joseph A. and Family
Owns Hispanic food business known as Goya Foods.

Valdez, Luis
Father of Chicano theater. Actor, director, playwright, filmmaker. Wrote and directed *La Bamba*.

Vargas, Elizabeth
Famous television newscaster, works for the *Today Show,* correspondent for *NOW with Tom Brokaw and Katie Couric, Nightly News.*

Velez, Carmelo E. "Tom"
Started CTA, Inc., an aerospace and defense system manufacturer. Supplied government with flight simulators.

Villanueva, Daniel D. and Family
Earned fortune in the television industry.

REAL PEOPLE—HISPANICS IN AMERICA TODAY

Real people have their own ways.
They have their own traditions.
They have their own beliefs.
History is in their hearts.

We are proud of this section. The people we interviewed have Cuban, Puerto Rican, Spanish, or Mexican backgrounds. Their lives and heritage tell the story of part of America's history. Some have come from Cuba to find a new life. Others came to the United States as migrant farm workers and improved their lives through education. Some came from families who were here even before the pilgrims. We chose people from all walks of life, professionals and nonprofessionals—people involved in government, business, education, and religion.

A group of fifth-graders made up questions to ask, because we wanted to know about the people and their families, traditions, and values. We asked them about their favorite childhood memories, their views on prejudice, and their family traditions, because we think that this is how we can understand each other better. Again and again, we heard familiar themes, such as that Hispanic families care for each other, have strong religious traditions, and have a strong desire to serve their country. Our real people shared their own feelings and let us explore their lives. As you read about them, remember that they are just like you and me, not made up or superheroes but normal, everyday people who are proud to be Americans.

TINO MENDEZ

If you meet Tino Mendez, you will be impressed with his dedication, bravery, friendliness, and sense of humor. He works hard to remind people what freedom is and how important it is to have. He also likes to encourage others to work to preserve America's freeeom.

Mr. Mendez was born in Cuba in 1944. He was an only child for a long time. When he was 12, his parents had a daughter. Two

Tino Mendez

years later, they had another son. He loved his little brother and sister very much. Mr. Mendez has many good qualities, especially his pride and his love of freedom. His family means everything to him.

In high school, Tino Mendez was a good student. He was involved with the school government and played basketball. His early life was just like that of any one of us, but then a big change took place. In 1959, there was a revolution on the small island of Cuba. Mr. Mendez felt the new government starting to control his town and high school. He decided that if he were to get

help for his people, he had two choices. He could either stay and try to change things or leave and hopefully return and fight for freedom. It was a painful decision, but he decided he had to leave.

You must realize how hard it would be to get up and leave your family. When he was 16, Mr. Mendez filled out many papers, and at 17, he took a plane from Cuba to Florida. There he became a refugee. He was in a strange country with a strange language that he hardly knew.

When Mr. Mendez got to the United States, he entered a Catholic Charities camp for children under 18 years of age. At the camp, a bishop came and took Mr. Mendez to Kansas, where he found a foster home.

Mr. Mendez went to Benedictine College in Atchison, Kansas, and there he studied math. During this time, he worked at many jobs to try to pay for his education. One of the jobs he had was working on the farm where he was living. He decided to quit that because he was almost killed by a tractor! He then began working at Taco Tico, a fast-food place. Then he found out

The Mendez Family

At age 17, Tino Mendez fled Cuba for the U.S.

about a job making a lot more money selling encyclopedias door to door. Mr. Mendez graduated from Benedictine College in three years. After that, he didn't have to work any more odd jobs. He went on to get his doctoral degree from the University of Colorado.

Mr. Mendez is now a math teacher at Metropolitan State College in Denver, Colorado. He is married to Mary Ann, who is a pediatric nurse at the National Jewish Hospital, and has two sons, Matthew and Mark.

Mr. Mendez's sons also think education is important. Both of them are in college. One plans to be a lawyer, the other, a doctor.

Mr. Mendez is very active in our government because he wants to make certain that our country remains free. He has served in public office and campaigned for many candidates and causes. He does this because he knows the sting of being controlled by the government. His goal is to make people happy by helping them to

remain free. His son, Matthew, told us that the best advice from his dad was to be yourself. Tino Mendez's family is very lucky.

BERNADETTE VIGIL

Bernadette Vigil is a strong individual. She has chosen to remain single and devote her life to preserving the traditions of her heritage through her works of art. Ms. Vigil works hard to bring out her Hispanic heritage in the things she paints. Her art contains a lot of historical and religious ideas. Much of her work is done to help people remember things from the Hispanic culture. Ms. Vigil's feelings about her Hispanic heritage can be seen in what she paints.

Ms. Vigil has lived in Santa Fe, New Mexico, since she was born in 1955. She has five brothers, one sister, and her mother and father, so there are nine people in her family. Her mom and dad taught her to respect other people, because that's the way you're going to want to be treated yourself.

Her parents taught her about religion and how it was very important. They also taught her to believe in herself. Her favorite holidays are religious ones, especially Easter and Christmas. She believes in her religion a lot, and her paintings show it. Many of her pictures have crosses, funerals, and resurrections in them.

Ms. Vigil grew up in a wonderful old part of Santa Fe, and her home was made of adobe. On the street where she lived, a lot of other artists lived. When she was little, she played with water snakes

Bernadette Vigil

and lizards. Her dream was to be a policewoman. That was because she liked the clothes they wore. By sixth or seventh grade, she knew she wanted to be a painter. That might be because several of her relatives were artists. Also, she would watch the artists on her street painting beautiful pictures.

Ms. Vigil always liked to draw, and her parents were very supportive. She liked art in school. After she graduated from high school, she went to New Mexico Highlands University. Later, she went to the College of Santa Fe and graduated.

Ms. Vigil's house is built on land that her grandparents homesteaded a long time ago. She doesn't plan to marry or have children. She said, "I always wanted to be an artist,

but being an artist is not a traditional role for a Hispanic woman, and in the Hispanic culture, having children is very important. This is my way of having a family. My paintings are a part of me. They are my children. They are my offspring, and I hope that they can inspire others in their lives."

Bernadette Vigil works all over New Mexico as a painter and really enjoys it. She likes to paint oils and frescoes, which are paintings on plaster.

We think Ms. Vigil sounds like a very nice and interesting person. New Mexico is neat, but with Bernadette Vigil there, it's neater.

SIDNEY ATENCIO

Sidney Atencio is the kind of person that people love to be around. He is kind, respectful, and funny. He has dark hair and a mustache. He is tanned and has a low voice, and he is big and very strong. He believes that all people should be respected regardless of their color or beliefs. He feels that his name is something special, and he's proud of it. To Mr. Atencio, learning to spell and say someone's name correctly is a sign of respect.

Mr. Atencio's relatives were some of the first people to come to the part of Mexico that is now the southern United States. This was even before the pilgrims landed on Plymouth Rock. The family that he grew up in was very small, with three children, but when his whole family got together, it was completely different. In fact, people would walk by and say, "Is that all one family?"

Mr. Atencio must believe in education,

because he has gone to school for 27 years. During the last four years of his schooling, he studied to be a deacon in the Catholic Church. Mr. Atencio adores books, and he works in the Denver Public Library.

Mr. Atencio loves family gatherings. We think he likes family gatherings so much because he is a deacon who helps people. He has been a deacon for four years. He works mainly with the homeless at the Samaritan Center. He counsels many people, such as husbands and wives with marriage problems, and much more.

Mr. Atencio has a family of his own. He has a wife and two sons named after famous Hispanics. His sons are called Francisco and

Deacon Sidney Atencio

Diego. His wife, Lillian, is a big part of his life. She works in the post office. (But it's not her fault the mail is late!)

An old tradition in the Hispanic Catholic Church is called *Quinceanera* (15th birthday). This is when a girl celebrates that she is becoming a woman. As girls approach the age of 15, they take preparation classes. In these classes, they talk about friendship, dating, drugs, suicide, and family communication. You don't have to be Hispanic to do this.

Mr. Atencio is carrying on this tradition by holding classes and preparing the girls and their families for this ceremony. It is very important to him that the girls learn about themselves and their culture. He feels this is a great way to keep tradition alive as well as to help the young girls lead healthier, happier lives. At the end of the classes, the girls' families and friends celebrate the Quinceanera. The girl wears a white dress like a bride, and each one has 14 escorts (like bridesmaids and groomsmen) who march in procession. During the mass, the girl has to make a speech called "Who Am I?" Her parents talk about her to the guests. Mr. Atencio said a lot of people cry because it is so beautiful. After the ceremony, the girl has officially turned "sweet 15."

Sidney Atencio spends a lot of his time teaching people to be proud of who they are. It is important to him that people know about themselves and their heritage and celebrate their beginnings. He wants people to pass on the traditions that they have through their families and their heritage.

BENNIE AND LIL RAZO

Bennie and Lil Razo live in Chillicothe, Illinois. Both of their families came from Mexico. We chose to talk to these people because their family life illustrates a very important part of the Hispanic heritage. They have a loving, caring, very close family. They have worked hard to keep close and show their family that happiness in life and family are the most important things to work for.

Mr. Razo's father, Thomas, came to the United States when his uncle got him a job working for the Santa Fe Railroad. Mr. Razo's uncle was a foreman on the railroad. Thomas moved to Chillicothe, where the railroad job was. Later, when his father married, he and his wife moved into a boxcar to live. The railroad company offered only boxcars for houses to people who hadn't worked for the company very long. If you had worked on the railroad for a long time, you could live in a brick house.

Bennie Razo was born in this boxcar and lived there until he was 18 years old. Then he joined the military and was sent to Korea. Mr. Razo later went to college, but before he could finish, he left because he needed to take care of his new family.

Mr. Razo married Lil. They had two girls and two boys. He now works as a custodian. Mrs. Razo is a housewife and also works on an assembly line. They taught their kids what their parents taught them. This was to show respect for everyone, especially their parents, and not to be ashamed of who you are.

When Mr. Razo was a kid, he liked going

to the movies with his parents once a month. When Mrs. Razo was a kid, she liked going to the country, taking long walks, picking blackberries, and playing games. She remembers that once when she was young, a boy teased her and her girlfriend about being Hispanic. Her brother came out of the house one day and scared him away. He never teased them again. Mrs. Razo doesn't think people are as prejudiced as they used to be.

Mr. Razo's hero was his high school coach, George Taylor. Coach Taylor was there for Mr. Razo when he had trouble in school. He made him stay in school even though it was difficult for him. The special people who helped Mr. Razo become who he is today are his dad and Coach Taylor. When Mr. Razo was in high school, he wanted to be a coach and a teacher.

Mrs. Razo's parents were married in Mexico. They worked their way north and eventually immigrated to the United States. This means they left their home in Mexico to live in the United States. Many people left their homelands because of wars or sickness. Sometimes they left for political or religious reasons. Mrs. Razo's family came to find better jobs. Her family paid a penny each to cross the border. This was a processing fee for paperwork.

As a young girl, Mrs. Razo wanted to be a cosmetologist when she grew up. Mrs. Razo's brother, Joe, was her hero because he taught her to stand up for herself and be proud of who she is. The special person who helped her become who she is today is her mother.

Today, Mr. and Mrs. Razo's four children are grown up and starting their own families. They have all worked hard to be what they are. Each one has spent time in school trying very hard to succeed in life. Jacqueline works in a bank. Renee works at the Area Agency on Aging, a state-funded program. Tom teaches in southern Illinois. David works in a restaurant and goes to college.

Ms. Razo's advice to Hispanic youth is to be proud of yourself and "go out in life and do the best you can." Mr. Razo's words of wisdom are, "Study, because no one can ever take your education away from you." Their goals are to live a happy life with a happy family, and they're doing just that! The Razos know they have been successful because now, as their children start their own lives, they, too, are working hard to carry on the family traditions.

PETE VALDEZ

We chose to write about Pete Valdez because he represents a good example for Hispanics in America. Mr. Valdez served our country by fighting in World War II as a member of the U.S. Army. It has been estimated that nearly 500,000 Hispanic people fought in World War II as part of the armed forces. Mr. Valdez has very strong feelings about our country and fought very hard to keep it the way it is.

Mr. Valdez was one of six people to win the Silver Helmet Award on April 21, 1991. He is the first Mexican American to win this award, which is a trophy that has a small,

Pete Valdez

shiny helmet about the size of a small clock on a thick dish. It is a replica of the G.I. steel helmet soldiers used in World War II. In fact, it looks just like the helmet Mr. Valdez used when he fought in the war.

The Silver Helmet Award for performing excellent service for our country is given by the AMVETS organization. This is an organization of American veterans of World War II, Korea, and Vietnam. The awards are given to people who have worked hard and made a difference in areas such as defense, patriotism, rehabilitation, congressional service, and peace. All people can be nominated for this award. The Silver Helmet Award is sometimes called the Oscar Award for veterans. That means that it is like the awards for movie stars, except it is for veterans.

Pete Valdez was born in Los Angeles, California. He is the oldest of 21 brothers and sisters. There are three sets of twins in his family. His family was poor. So they could earn money for the family, Pete and his brother would shine shoes for the people who got off the boats at the docks. He and his brother would hide their shoeshine kits behind the bushes while they were at school, because they didn't want to take them into the school. When they got out of school, they would go to the boats. Pete and his brother would also make money by picking up bananas and wood that dropped from the crates that came from the boats. They put both things in their little red wagon and sold them for nickels and dimes. They would also sell newspapers at the dock.

Pete's dad worked full-time as a stevedore (someone who works on docks loading ships) and part-time as a mechanic. Pete used to help his father in the garage. His hands would get all greasy. He scrubbed and scrubbed, but he couldn't get his hands clean. Other kids used to tease him about being dirty. Pete would fight or run away.

When he was a little boy, Mr. Valdez wanted to be a tank driver. He was so interested in this job that he enlisted in the army when he was 17. He went to tank-driving school in Ft. Hood, Texas. He was very happy to go to tank school, but then he had some bad luck. One day when he was in school, they called 15 people out. He was one of them. Mr. Valdez got the news that he was going to the South Pacific to man a machine gun. He never got to drive a tank, but he was proud to serve his country. He was lucky and got out of the war without a scratch.

After World War II, Mr. Valdez knew he needed an education. So, when he got home, he applied for the G.I. Bill to go to school. The government created this bill to set aside money for military people to be retrained after they left the service. Mr. Valdez learned to work in a machine shop and design tools, and got a job in a machine shop. He also was the security guard. When he had extra time at night, Mr. Valdez would learn how to use each machine. After one year, Mr. Valdez went to work at Hughes Aircraft. He worked his way up until he was a project manager. Then he started hiring people from Hispanic neighborhoods to work at Hughes.

Mr. Valdez married his high-school sweetheart, who was his next door neighbor. Her name is Rosie. Marrying Rosie was a tremendous help. Mr. Valdez says that she is the "light of his life." Mr. and Mrs. Valdez had four sons. They all wanted to be in the service. Three got to serve. The other one really wanted to serve, too, but didn't get to because he had medical problems. Now

he's a minister. Two of the sons served in the Army, and the other served in the Air Force.

Mr. Valdez is a proud American who has contributed in many ways to his country and his family. He fought in World War II and then came back to help other soldiers who fought in wars. He volunteers many, many hours to make our country a good place. Because we think Mr. Valdez is special, his advice is important to us. He believes the family is important and wants everyone to respect their parents and elders. He told us to be honest with everyone and to try very hard to get an education so you can make more of yourself.

ALICIA FERNANDEZ-MOTT

We talked with Alicia Fernandez-Mott, a very important advocate for migrant farm workers. She is a supervisor for the Division of Migrant and Seasonal Farmworker Programs, with the U.S. Department of Labor in Washington, D.C. She works with the Job Training Partnership Act. This act is meant to provide education for adult farm workers so they can get year-round and full-time work.

Alicia Fernandez-Mott was a migrant worker herself for several years. In doing her job as an advocate for migrant farm workers, she met both Cesar Chavez and Baldamar Velasquez, who is the president of the Farm Labor Organizing Committee. Both of these people worked hard to get migrant farm workers a lot of the services they need and deserve, like health care and

Alicia Fernandez-Mott

clean facilities in which to live. Ms. Fernandez-Mott is proud of the work she has done with Mr. Chavez and Mr. Baldamar in helping the farm workers. Because she herself has lived as a migrant farm worker, she shares the strength and determination these men brought to their work.

Alicia traveled with her family along the migrant streams from the age of four, off and on, until she was 20. She actually started working at the age of six by picking tomatoes and cucumbers. This was hard work because she wasn't very strong.

Because she dropped out of school at the age of 16, Ms. Fernandez-Mott has had to work very hard to get where she is now. She went back to school when she was 30.

She received her G.E.D. (that means high school equivalency diploma) and then went to college. She got her degree in business.

Ms. Fernandez-Mott had lots of information about migrant farm workers. This is just some of what she shared with us.

Migrant farm workers are people who have a very determined work ethic resulting from having to earn their keep.

They are people who have very little education or work skills. Most migrant workers don't speak English, so they have a difficult time finding a job. They work as migrant farm workers because they don't need to speak fluent English and they don't need to have any schooling. Since this kind of job keeps a person moving, it is next to impossible to get any education or skills to learn a different job. So these people end up being migrant workers forever. The kids end up in the same situation as their parents, since they don't have an education or skills.

Working as a migrant farm worker is a very difficult situation. These workers travel in migrant streams, or routes to different harvest places that workers follow. They travel in crowded trucks. Sometimes the workers travel with their families, but other times they are separated. The trucks are filled with people of all ages. Sometimes they travel for two and a half to three days straight. The workers don't know much about where they go. They judge the distance by state borders, not by miles. When they stop at their farms to work, the workers are packed tight into small cabins that don't always have indoor plumbing.

They are supposed to have a refrigerator, but often it doesn't work. Small propane stoves are also supplied, but the migrant workers have to supply the propane fuel, and sometimes they can't afford it.

There are a lot of health problems that come with the job. There are pesticides that can harm people. Pesticides hurt your lungs, eyes, and skin. The type of labor involved requires a lot of stooping, bending, and lifting. All of these movements can hurt the joints in your body. There are a few clinics for the workers, but these are not free, and a lot of the time, the workers can't afford them. Also, these clinics don't cover all of the problems that the workers might have. They are limited in what they can cure. A lot of the health problems of farm workers go uncared for.

Migrant workers are paid by how much they pick. Their employers pay them a certain amount of money for each basket or bushel of food they gather. The amount of money they make is different at each stop. If the crops are good, then they will earn more money. Since their earnings are so uncertain, farm workers can't save money. They also don't get extra money to cover the cost of gas to get from one place to another.

Ms. Fernandez-Mott has been helping migrant workers so they won't face the problems she did with getting an education so that she could get a better-paying job. She works hard to set up programs for training and other kinds of education. If the parents get educated, then their children don't have to travel all the time. They can afford more things and can also receive their own education. She is very determined to show Hispanic people how to set goals and measure their achievements. Ms. Fernandez-Mott feels Hispanic people need more education to earn respect in American society. She also wants to show other people about Hispanic heritage and its value to the United States.

SYLVIA TELLES RYAN

Sylvia Telles Ryan is a person who has spent her whole life helping people. This takes faith, courage, and love, which she has found in the roots of her family's past.

Three flags have flown over New Mexico. They are the Spanish flag, the Mexican flag, and now the American flag. Ms. Ryan's ancestors have been there the whole time. They were the settlers, ranchers, deputies, ditch riders, and ordinary people of their time. Her family never moved to America. The land they owned became the United States territory in 1848. Even though the American flag flew over the land, her family were not considered citizens. They were still called subjects under the king of Spain.

Ms. Ryan's great-grandfather on her dad's side was a cattle rancher east of Las Cruces, New Mexico. Her mother's grandfather owned a ranch next to a lake named after them—Lucero Lake. The original farmhouse is still on this property and can be seen today with special permission of the U.S. government. It is near the White Sands National Monument.

Sylvia Telles Ryan

Ms. Ryan's ancestors did many great things. Her great-uncle was the sheriff of Las Cruces in 1908 when Pat Garrett, the man who shot Billy the Kid, was killed over a land dispute by Wayne Brazel. You can read all about Wayne Brazel surrendering to Sheriff Lucero in history books today.

Ms. Ryan has a mom and dad, a brother, and three sisters. They all grew up in Las Cruces. They were brought up with a deep respect for their family, their religion, and their elders. She remembers a time when her dad was having a special guest over. Ms. Ryan's dad made her practice how to greet his friend. She pretended her dad was the guest and practiced and practiced until she could do it right. When the man came, she gave him a very respectful greeting.

Ms. Ryan was taught to be respectful to older people in her family, too. When her

Uncle Margarito was around, he would ask her to get him a glass of water, and she would go directly to the kitchen. She would walk back to her uncle and stand next to him with her arms folded. When her uncle was finished, she would return the glass to the kitchen.

They had some special neighbors named Marquez, who owned a tortilla factory. Some afternoons, Grandma Marquez would have them kneel and pray the rosary with her. If they were all behaving while she took care of them, occasionally they were allowed to go to the tortilla factory. There they would get a hot tortilla with butter on it! Another thing Ms. Ryan's parents shared with her was their faith, but she was not always as close to God as she is now. When she was in college, she went on a church "Teen Day," and she heard some people from her school talking about God. She then realized how important she thought God really was.

Ms. Ryan lives in St. Paul, Minnesota, today. She works for the National Evangelization Teams (NET). In 1987, she volunteered for ten months to travel with other people and talk to youth about God. Then she was hired in 1988 to help train the NET people. Ms. Ryan has even traveled to Australia for her work. She is very grateful and excited because NET is beginning to work with more Hispanics. They have a team that went to Honduras this year, and they work in areas of the United States where there are many Hispanic people. Ms. Ryan really has a heart for what she calls her *raza* (race).

In 1992, Ms. Ryan met and married Tom Ryan, who also works for NET. In 1993, Thomas Jr. was born. His brother, Matthew, came along two years later. Ms. Ryan continues to volunteer for NET.

THE MARTINEZ FAMILY

Martinez is a very common name in Hispanic culture. Today, there are four generations alive in this one Martinez family of 75 members, which began with Maria and Juan Martinez. All of them live less than 150 miles from each other in the state of Colorado. By interviewing seven members of this extended family, we were able to see the changes each generation made through time with things like traditions, education, careers, and holidays.

The first generation is Maria Martinez, the great-grandmother. Next we talked to her daughter, Odelia Martinez Quintana, and her son, Jose Martinez. They are the second generation. For the third generation, we interviewed Diana Quintana Martinez and Jose Martinez Jr. The fourth generation is made up of Jose III and Julio, who are Maria Martinez's great-grandchildren.

The First Generation

Maria Martinez was born on April 6, 1909, in a small town in New Mexico. She remembers always wanting to play, but she always had a lot of work to do. Maria went to a very small school until the third grade, when she left school to help at home with the family.

When Maria was 16, she married Juan P. Martinez, who was 27 years old. Mr. and Mrs. Martinez had some land in New Mexico where they raised their children before coming to Colorado. In a very small home they had 14 children. Two of the 14 children died. The older children helped their mother take care of the younger children.

Mr. and Mrs. Martinez moved from New Mexico to Colorado with their family. Shortly after this time, Mr. Martinez died. Some of the kids wanted to finish high school, but they were not able to because they had to work and help support the family. The family always came first in the Martinez home.

Maria's home is close to some of her children. The home is decorated with many pictures of her family. There are also many statues and pictures of saints. Mrs. Martinez does a lot of things the same way she did when she lived in her small home in New Mexico. She washes her clothes by hand and hangs them on her clothesline. She makes her own special type of beef jerky and hangs it in a bedroom to dry. She still makes all of her own tortillas and breads from scratch and still cans fruits and vegetables. Maria says she has lived a very full life and that she is very happy. We hope she lives for many more years.

The Second Generation

Odelia Martinez was born in 1928. She is Mrs. Martinez's oldest living daughter. Odelia went to school until she was 14.

The family tree of the Maria and Juan Martinez family

After leaving school, she moved to Denver with her cousins and got a job. When she was 21 years old, she married Ben Quintana. They had three kids, named David, Thomas, and Diana.

Mr. Quintana worked as a mechanic, and Mrs. Quintana stayed home to care for her kids. Once the Quintanas wanted a new car seat for their car, so they made it all by themselves. Other people liked the work they did and asked if they could make cushions and seat covers for them. The word spread about their good work, and soon Mr. Quintana quit his job to begin the new business with Mrs. Quintana. This business, called Ben's Upholstery, is still run by their family today in Denver, Colorado! Mrs. Quintana must be pretty smart to have a family and a good career at the same time.

Mrs. Quintana and her husband still live in the same house they bought when they were first married. Just like her mother, she still cans her own fruits and vegetables and makes her own tortillas. When we asked her if there was something about her past that she would change if she could, she said that she would like to have known how to borrow more money when she was

starting her business. She is a very happy person and is very proud of her family.

Jose Martinez was born in 1936. He is one of Mrs. Martinez's seven sons and a brother to Maria. One of his favorite memories is when he and his brothers and sisters played with homemade guitars.

Mr. Martinez went to school until he was in the eighth grade. He then went to work on a farm. When he was 19 years old, he got married to Altagracia Baca, who was 18. Jose and Altagracia had four kids. Mr. Martinez went back to school to get his G.E.D. Later, Mr. Martinez became the manager of a farm. His job helped his wife to go back to school, too, and earn her G.E.D. After she got her diploma, she went to college to become a teacher. Mr. Martinez is now a field worker for a chemical company. He belongs to the Knights of Columbus and is always ready to help the community. Mrs. Martinez is a teacher in an elementary school. Mr. Martinez had advice for us. He said to stay in school. He wished that he had stayed in school when he was younger.

The Third Generation

Diana Quintana was born in 1960. She is the youngest of three children. When she was growing up, she helped her mother with the chores at home and at her parents' business. She also played in a nearby creek catching bugs and play-acting the Miss America Pageant with friends. She says her childhood was lots

of fun. She remembers celebrating Christmas with a decorated tree and waiting for Santa Claus to come and leave gifts.

When she graduated from high school, she got married to Michael Martinez and went to college for one year. She is now an office manager for an insurance company. Diana doesn't have any children, but she and her husband have traveled quite a bit since they got married.

Jose Martinez Jr. was born in 1958. When he was a little boy, he helped his father on the farm feeding the cattle and riding on the tractors. He was in Boy Scouts and played baseball. He says that he had a very happy childhood.

Jose Jr. grew up believing that Santa Claus came on December 25 to leave gifts for good boys and girls. He did not know about the Three Kings and January 6. He wants to help his own kids understand how religion and Christmas go together, and he is trying to help them celebrate the Day of the Three Kings.

Jose Jr. finished high school and college. Then he married Annette Acevedo and had two children, Jose III and Julio. He was the first person in his family to graduate from college. Jose Jr. says that he has more opportunities in his life than his father did. He is now a counselor in a high school and has a master's degree.

The things that are the most important to Jose Jr. are health, family, education, and remembering where you came from, so that you can be as good a person as possible.

Standing left to right: Odelia Martinez Quintana, Diana Quintana, Jose D. Martinez I, Jose A. Martinez II; Sitting: Julio R. Martinez, Maria Martinez, Jose A. Martinez III

The Fourth Generation

Jose III (born in 1985) and Julio (born in 1988) are the sons of Jose Martinez Jr. They are learning from their parents the importance of their heritage. As young as the boys are, they are already saving for college. Jose III and Julio say, "If you want to be cool, stay in school."

Changes over the Four Generations

Families have gotten smaller in number. They have acquired degrees in higher education, and careers have changed. There are more choices for both men and women.

Holidays are still celebrated and still have some of the same traditions they did 80 years ago!

BISHOP ROBERTO GONZALES

Many Hispanics are gaining leadership roles across our country. Bishop Roberto Gonzales, a leader in the Roman Catholic Church, became a bishop at the young age of 38 years old.

Bishop Gonzales was born in Elizabeth, New Jersey, on June 2, 1950. Although he was born in New Jersey, he grew up in San Juan, Puerto Rico. He came from a very large family. There are nine kids in his family. He is the oldest. With his parents, that is a total of 11 people. He has many aunts, cousins, and uncles, too.

Like most of us, Bishop Gonzales has a hero, but it's not Rambo, Superman, or Batman. The bishop's hero was his father, because he always knew what was going on in the family, and he was around when the family needed him. The bishop said that his father had a ton of love for the family.

His mother's grandmother, Carmen Nieves, was also a very special person to him. She taught Bishop Gonzales and his brothers and sisters to take care of the graves of their relatives. They kept the graves pretty by pulling weeds and planting more flowers. This is very important to the people in Puerto Rico. It is part of a tradition that helps people remember that family love goes beyond life. Just because someone isn't here doesn't mean you can't still show them

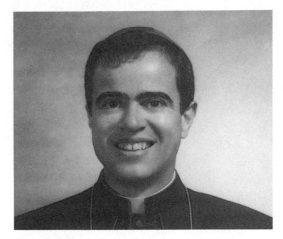

Bishop Roberto Gonzales

love and respect. They do this by cleaning the graves and respecting their burial sites.

Some of the favorite holidays that the Gonzales family celebrated were Christmas, New Year's, festival days, and also Holy Thursday. On Holy Thursday, Bishop Gonzales' father would read the passage of the Last Supper from the Bible. After reading the Bible, the family would eat lamb and matzo (matzo is bread made without yeast), and each child would get a small sip of wine. The bishop also likes the tradition called the nine days of Christmas. During this time people go to church at 5:00 in the morning and sing Christmas folk songs in church. After church, the whole family drinks hot chocolate. This celebration is called *Misa de Aginaldo*. Puerto Ricans say that it is like a gift to go to church.

When he was little, the bishop wanted to be a doctor, a lawyer, and a police officer, just like other kids, but by the time he

was 14, he knew he wanted to be a priest. In 1964, he went to New York to a Franciscan seminary. He finished high school, went to college and then to theology school. After he was a priest, he studied sociology at Fordham University in New York City. Now, at age 41, Roberto Gonzales is a Roman Catholic bishop in Weston, Massachusetts, which is a town west of Boston.

In 1995, Pope John Paul II appointed Bishop Gonzales Coadjutor Bishop of Corpus Christi, Texas. This means that when the current bishop retires, Bishop Gonzales will take his place.

Bishop Gonzales feels that all languages are God's languages, and that you should be proud of your culture. He says, "Love your roots, love yourselves, love your family, and love all people." We think he is a great Hispanic leader.

HOMERO E. ACEVEDO II

Homero E. Acevedo II is an executive with the American Telephone and Telegraph Company (AT&T). Mr. Acevedo has used his good education and his ability to communicate well in English and Spanish to become one of the youngest managers of the AT&T National Bilingual Center in San Antonio, Texas. There are lots of things we can learn from Mr. Acevedo.

Mr. Acevedo is very close to his family. Born in 1961, he is the youngest child. His family includes his late father, Homero Sr., his mother, Maria, his two sisters, Annette and Angelique, and his twin brothers, Hugo and Hector.

When Mr. Acevedo was young, he was never lonesome with his brothers and sisters around. He especially remembers going down the stairs Christmas morning, when his father made home movies and blinded him with bright floodlights.

His father and mother always encouraged him to get a good education, share with others, love others, work hard, and be all that he could be. They were also a good example for him. His parents were and still are his heroes.

Mr. Acevedo's parents gave him advice about how to handle teasing and prejudice. His father told him that if someone thought there was something wrong with him because he was Hispanic, then that person must not have been educated very well and should be ignored. So that is exactly what he has done. He is proud of who he is.

Mr. Acevedo's dad taught him what goals are and helped him achieve some. One of his goals was to become an outstanding athlete. He did, and his favorite sports were soccer, baseball, and basketball. At one point, he played semiprofessional soccer. He loves Chicago teams, especially the Bears, Bulls, Cubs, and Blackhawks. Although sports are an important part of Mr. Acevedo's life, they never became his main goal.

The most important goal was to get a good education. Mr. Acevedo realized that a good education would open many doors for him in the future. In high school, he studied hard and made excellent grades.

He then graduated from the University of Denver. While in college, he had a chance to study in Spain. By being one of the top academic students, he got to meet the king of Spain, Juan Carlos.

Mr. Acevedo knew that he needed to be ready to move to different parts of the country to advance in his career. He moved to New Jersey for training. He was in charge of testing a new billing system and a new computer system that would take care of 80 million residential customer accounts. This was a great responsibility, and Mr. Acevedo took it seriously.

After six months of testing the computer system, he was moved to San Antonio, Texas. There he is an operations manager in charge of the International Communications Service Center. Many office managers report to him. There are about 175

Homero E. Acevedo II (left) and family.

people in his department. He makes sure that everything runs smoothly.

Mr. Acevedo is able to communicate with people very well. He can speak and write fluent English and Spanish. He feels very lucky to know two languages and believes it has helped him be a successful executive. He says, "Anyone can be a success if they are secure with themselves, ready to move, and an achiever." This is the motto Mr. Acevedo lives by.

In 1994, Mr. Acevedo met and married Rita Velasquez. Their first baby, Sarina Isabella, was born in 1995.

MARY ANN A. ZAPATA

Mary Ann Zapata has dedicated her life to education. She not only worked hard to overcome obstacles and get a good education, but now she works to help others achieve the same things.

As a teacher, she is a very catchy woman! She catches children's attention by telling them about how she was raised and how to get a good education. She teaches her students to get along with one another, to stay in school, and not to judge people by their color or race.

Can you imagine moving almost every year? As a child, Mary Ann Zapata grew up in a family of migrant farm workers. If you're wondering what a migrant family is, it is a family that moves a lot. The family moves a lot because crops ripen at different times of the year, so the family must go to different farms to work, even if they are in other states.

Mary Ann A. Zapata

Mary Ann was born on November 25, 1943, in Texas. When she was four, she moved to Walla Walla, Washington. Each year, her family moved to Oregon and then to California. Then she and her family moved back to Walla Walla because that was like their home base.

When Mary Ann was in first grade, the teacher showed prejudice and did not like her. Mary Ann only knew how to speak Spanish. The teacher ignored her and did not want to teach her how to speak English. Even the kids were mean. They teased her and also made faces and called her names. She had only one friend in first grade. However, the other kids told Mary Ann's friend that she was Hispanic and to stop being her friend, so soon she had no friends. Then she did not want to go to school, but her parents made her go anyway. In second grade, the teacher was warmer and kinder and taught her to speak English. When Mary Ann was older, she wanted to be a teacher because she didn't want kids to be treated poorly.

Is your father your hero? Mrs. Zapata's father was, and still is, her hero. When she learned English, she wanted to teach her parents. Since her father had to work, she would read to him every night. If you are wondering why her dad is her hero, it is because his opinions helped her to get a good education and to stay in school. He would take her out into the field and show her how tough life would be if she did not get a good education by staying in school.

Mrs. Zapata's favorite holidays have

always been Christmas and Easter. She likes spending time with her family and relatives and has realized the importance of family.

Mrs. Zapata and her husband, Julio, have five daughters. The oldest is married, the two youngest still live at home, and the other two are off at college. Her daughters' ages are 10, 13, 19, 23, and 25. Mrs. Zapata teaches her kids to get along, not to judge people by their looks, and to remember to treat other people the way you would like to be treated.

Mrs. Zapata went to college to learn how to be a teacher because her younger years were uncomfortable. She went to college for five years and is still going so she can learn more about how to be a better teacher. She feels sadness in her heart when she hears somebody is going to drop out of school. Mrs. Zapata is now the bilingual consultant for teachers and students. She was also responsible for translating the school handbook into Spanish to help Hispanic parents understand what happens at school.

CARLOS FLORES, M.D.

Are you proud of being Hispanic? Well, Dr. Carlos Flores is! Don't you think it would be exhausting to be an emergency medicine doctor, taking care of people who come to the hospital emergency room for help? This is exactly what Carlos Flores, M.D. does.

Dr. Flores explained that it took a lot of hard work and ambition to get where he is today. When he was in ninth grade, he

Dr. Carlos Flores

got very interested in biology, and that is when he set his goal to become a doctor. He went to Northwestern University in Chicago for four years and studied very hard as a pre-med student. Then he went to medical school at New York University for four more years. After that, he did two years of residency and additional training in emergency medicine. He has been an emergency medicine doctor for seven years in the New York City area. He says he still has to continue to read and learn about all of the new advances and discoveries in his field.

Dr. Flores' job involves many different kinds of medicine. He does everything from helping with sore throats and ear infections, to diagnosing broken bones and taking care of people who have been in accidents or have had heart attacks. His most memorable experience was when a girl was having a very bad asthma attack. She wasn't breathing very well and was turning blue. Dr. Flores helped bring her pink color back, and she was able to breathe well again.

Carlos Flores was born February 23, 1956. He forgets how quickly time flies. During our interview, his wife laughed at him because often it seemed to him as if something happened two years ago, when it was really ten. He grew up in a suburb of San Juan, Puerto Rico, and went to George O. Robinson School from kindergarten through 12th grade. When he was younger, he liked to play basketball. His idol and hero as a kid was Jerry West, who was one of the L.A. Lakers' basketball players. He had a friend named Billy, and they stayed at each other's houses every other weekend. He was also an Eagle Scout, which is the highest level in Boy Scouting, and he went to two jamborees, which are big Boy Scout meetings. One was in Idaho, and the other was in Japan.

Although he is the only child of his parents, Cristina and Carlos, he grew up with a very large extended family. This includes about 40 cousins, aunts, and uncles. As a boy, he liked to travel with his parents to the United States. His parents speak Spanish and English. He would like to teach his children Spanish.

Dr. Flores lived in Puerto Rico from 1956 to 1982. His ancestors lived in Puerto Rico also. In Puerto Rico, Dr. Flores and his family did not have any problems with prejudiced people because almost everybody there is Hispanic. However, he says being Puerto Rican affected his life when he went away to college. There he had to overcome the prejudice some people had against Hispanics. Dr. Flores proved them wrong by just being himself, and they soon found out that he was just like one of them.

Dr. Flores now lives in the New York City area. He is married and has two small boys. His wife is Jewish, so his family celebrates all the Jewish holidays as well as Christmas, New Year's, and the Day of the Three Kings. His favorite foods are rice and beans and pasta. Although he does not have any hobbies, he does a lot of work around the house, such as redoing the bathroom and rebuilding the backyard deck. He also likes to spend time with his children and his wife. Dr. Flores says that his goals are to be a good father and husband and to be the best doctor he can be.

Dr. Flores' advice to others is to stay in school, set goals, and don't let anyone stop you.

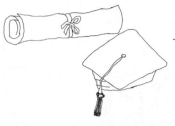

YOUNG PEOPLE WHO MAKE A DIFFERENCE

These young people love to care,
Spreading love and laughter everywhere.
They work hard and use their minds,
Helping all of humankind.

 Young heroes are people who put others before themselves. When most people think of their hero, they think of someone who is famous, rich, or well-known. But true heroes often don't have money or fame. Opportunities to help others and to do the right thing come naturally for these people. In this chapter, we look at the lives of six young heroes. These heroes are important to their communities and they set an example for others.

The heroes in this part of the book are young people who give their time to help. They set goals and they volunteer to serve in hospitals, churches, and schools. Some heroes teach swimming lessons, clean up neighborhoods, or make their community a safer place to live in.

We hope this part of the book gives you ideas about how you can become a young hero, too. By starting out small and setting goals, you can make a difference and be a young hero to the world. Remember that heroes are usually everyday people who lead regular lives. Each one is unique.

Ismael Hernandez

ISMAEL HERNANDEZ

In the spring of 1991, when Ismael Hernandez was 13 years old, he saved a young girl from drowning. That's one of the reasons "Ish" is a young hero. "To be a hero, you have to think fast," he says, "and think about the person in need." Ish was watching *911*—his favorite TV program—when he heard screams for help outside his townhouse. The cries came from Avani Patel, a ten-year-old girl, who had been biking near the flooded Prairie Creek. Her brother had accidentally bumped her back tire, and she fell in the creek. She was struggling to get out.

Ish quickly ran back into his house and got his brother Armando to help, too. Then he raced back to the creek and jumped in. The water was up to his chest, and his feet got stuck in the mud. He was horrified to see the now unconscious girl floating toward the drain pipe. The strong current was pulling her under, and she was dan-gerously close to the drain pipe. Ish knew that the drain pipe went under the street for almost a mile!

Swimming through the water, Ish pushed hard to reach Avani and pull her to the side of the creek. With the help of Armando, he lifted Avani out of the water. The paramedics resuscitated her and took her to the hospital. Fortunately, Ish had reached her in time. She only spent one night in the hospital.

Later, the media arrived. Reporters wanted to hear his story. That night he received several phone calls from friends, news stations—even from the television program *911*. Ish's story was in the papers and on TV the next day. All the publicity made Ish feel like a hero, but it also made him uncomfortable. He even declined an offer to be on *911*.

After the accident, Ish and several other neighbors attended town meetings. They tried to persuade the city officials to cover the drainage pipe or put a fence around the area. The officials refused. They thought that both ideas were too expensive. But people in the area haven't given up. They still hope to find a way to prevent future tragedies.

Ismael lives with his parents, Nina and David, his older brother, Jose, and his two younger brothers, Armando and Javier. His mother and father were born in Mexico, but he and his brothers were all born in the United States. He is proud of both his Mexican and his American heritages.

Ish has had to make other brave choices in his life, too. Once, he was parking his car when two guys started a fight with him. Ish was stabbed in the shoulder. After this frightening incident, he was glad that his parents decided to move the family somewhere else. It was hard to leave his friends, but he wanted his younger brothers to be safe.

We think Ish is a hero because he got involved when someone needed his help. In his own words, "You can't think about yourself if you want to be a hero." True heroes like Ish make a big difference in the world.

SARAH RAMOS

Sarah was gripping her valedictorian speech nervously. While her hands were shaking, thousands of people were looking at her. Her speech was clear and strong—surprising even herself. At the end, the audience applauded. Sarah was so happy that

Sarah Ramos

tears ran down her face. When it was all over, Sarah was sad to leave her friends from high school. Then she started to think of all the new friends she was going to make at Stanford University, her new school. She saw an exciting life in front of her, but getting to this point hadn't been easy. Sarah remembered her school days and the years of hard work.

Sarah was in junior high school when she decided to try for a scholarship to college. She wanted to go to a good college, so she tried to get all A's in her classes. It wasn't easy! She spent about five hours studying every night. She often skipped lunch to get more work done, and she didn't watch TV very often. It took dedication for Sarah to get to the top of her class and earn those scholarships.

Even though Sarah had to give up some fun activities, she wouldn't quit her volunteer work. Sarah was the vice-president of the student council, and she worked hard to get other students involved in community service, too. She encouraged her peers to visit senior citizens in retirement homes or to help older people by shoveling snow.

She also took over the food drive at Northglenn High School because in the past it hadn't been successful. Sarah wanted to do something to change that. She made the food drive into a competition, and the school collected 8,000 pounds of canned and dried foods. There was so much food that the Salvation Army didn't have enough trucks to haul it away. Some of the students had to use their own trucks!

When she was younger, Sarah didn't always listen to her parents' advice. As she got older, she realized that her parents' ideas were worth listening to. She found that talking to them helped her make better decisions. Now Sarah goes to them for advice all the time. Her family is important to her.

Sarah's uncle is one of her heroes. He was the only child in her father's family to graduate from college and become a doctor. She has thought about following in his footsteps. She decided to volunteer at a local hospital, to see if she really wanted to be a doctor.

For the last two years, Sarah has volunteered every Sunday at St. Anthony's Hospital. She changes sheets, gets people water, gives people baths, and shaves men's faces. She takes patients for walks, helps them eat, and makes them feel comfortable. Sarah also help the nurses by talking to the patients in Spanish when they don't speak English. Sarah is not paid for her work, but she gets lots of smiles. Her volunteer work has touched peoples' lives in many special ways. In the past two years, Sarah has put in nearly 400 hours working at the hospital.

We think Sarah is a hero, and others must think so, too. One Hispanic organization gave her a gold medal and a $3,000 scholarship to college for being a good role model, combining hard work at school with community service. Today, Sarah is studying to be a doctor at Stanford University in California. We think she will be a great doctor. She is smart, and she really cares about people. These are qualities a doctor needs.

RICK ALIRE

Rick Alire is a strong-willed person. He knows you can accomplish anything if you work hard. He believes in standing up for himself and speaking his mind. Rick is already accomplishing some of his goals. One important goal is to help other people.

Some high school seniors spend their afternoons playing basketball, earning money, or just hanging out. But every afternoon, after his last class, Rick grabs a quick lunch and heads to Porter Memorial Hospital. Rick has many different jobs at the hospital. He takes patients to their rooms, makes their beds, alphabetizes files, and delivers flowers. He even helped put a cast on a patient's leg. He does whatever is needed and tries to be very helpful. Rick says volunteering is interesting and it keeps him busy. Someday he wants to be a doctor.

Rick also works for a program called the Fenix Center. This program talks to kids about HIV and other sexually transmitted diseases, and about pregnancy. It encourages kids to wait to have sex until they are married. As part of the program, Rick and other young people perform skits about sharing feelings and dealing with peer pressure.

Rick is a swimming instructor, as well. Instead of teaching ordinary swimming classes, though, he teaches kids with special needs. Rick smiles from one ear to the other when his students reach their goals.

In 1994, Rick Alire was chosen to receive one of the nine "Kids Who Care" awards. This award is presented by the Channel 9 TV station to only nine kids in their view-

Rick Alire

ing area. This special honor was given to Rick because of all his volunteer work. He received $900, as well as the happiness that comes from knowing that his work is appreciated.

Rick knows what it's like to deal with tough family situations. His father had a problem with alcohol. He hated seeing his dad taken away in an ambulance. When Rick was nine, his parents separated. Rick helped out with his little brother, Ramon, and his sister, Billie Marie, by checking their homework and getting them ready for bed.

Rick really admires his mom, Cathy Alire. She works hard to keep the family together, and has given up a lot so that her children might have more. Rick also enjoys church

and he knows many people there. He also helps his aunt teach classes to younger kids who are getting ready to receive their first communion.

Rick's family is very creative. They like to do art projects and learn best by example. Rick says that making things helps him think and relax. He also enjoys leather work. He likes making wallets, checkbook covers, and eyeglass cases. He even sells some of his crafts.

Dealing with his father's alcoholism has made Rick realize that alcohol abuse is horrible. His true friends know that he doesn't drink alcohol, and they don't bug him about it. He is committed to not drinking because if he starts, he feels he might become an alcoholic. Rick believes that alcohol abuse robbed him of his father, and he never wants his children to go through that.

We think Rick is a hero. He is devoted to his beliefs, his family, and his community. He is an excellent role model for others.

MARY RODAS

Imagine having your own job at the age of four and being vice-president of a toy company at age 13. This is what happened to Mary Rodas. Now, at 18, Mary earns $200,000 a year.

Her parents arrived in the U.S. in 1971, knowing very little English. Four years later, Mary Rodas was born on Christmas day. Her father worked as a building superintendent and her mother cleaned houses part time.

As a girl, she used to follow her dad

around on the job. One day they walked into the apartment of Donald Spector, a businessman at the Catco Toy Company. He was putting new tile on his kitchen floor. Four-year-old Mary noticed that the tiles on the floor weren't matching correctly. She pointed out the mistake to Mr. Spector. He was impressed with her bold honesty and her sharp eye. He decided to have her try out some of his toys. Later she became a toy consultant because she had such good suggestions about how to improve them.

Mary has a lot of good ideas. She thought up the idea of packaging CDs in various shapes like Santa Claus and Frosty the Snowman, so that they can be used as Christmas tree ornaments. Then she convinced Catco to put neon Hawaiian decorations on their white "Balzac Balloon Ball." Now the Balzac Balloon Ball is their most popular product. Another time, Mary convinced Catco to leave a beauty mark off a

doll that they were making. She thought it looked like a pimple. No doubt, that decision increased the number of dolls sold.

After being named vice-president of marketing for Catco, Mary had trouble keeping up with her school work. When she got to high school, she was treated badly because her classmates were jealous of her. She often had to be at work when she was supposed to be at school. Mary ended up transferring to the Professional Children's School in New York. This school is especially for kids who work. At this school, Mary's schedule was more flexible and she was able to balance school and work. She even found time to help the March of Dimes raise money for children with special needs.

Mary is now attending New York University, where she is studying film. Lots of people wonder why she wants to go to college when she already has such a good career. She thinks that it is important to keep learning new things, helping others, and spending time with friends.

Mary has taught us that, at a very young age, people can still make a difference. Her honesty and willingness to tell the truth let her live out the dream of many children.

BRIAN ROYBAL

The evening had finally arrived. Brian Roybal felt strange standing in front of hundreds of people who were honoring him as an outstanding student and volunteer. It seemed impossible that he was the only teenage boy receiving the highest award at the "Annual Hispanic Salute."

Later, we enjoyed listening to Brian tell us some of the things that are important to him. "I am proud to be Chicano," he says. "A Chicano knows where he comes from and is proud of it. A good Chicano helps not only Chicanos, but any group of people who are less privileged. As a Chicano, I believe that if everybody could understand one another better, there would be less crime and poverty." Brian is doing his part to help others and make his community a better place to live in.

When he started high school, Brian made an important decision. He had heard about the International Baccalaureate Program at George Washington High School in his town. It was supposed to be very difficult, and he wasn't even sure he

Brian Roybal

wanted to go there. But his parents encouraged him, even though many kids quit. When he finished, he received a full tuition scholarship to a good engineering school. All his hard work had been worth it! Now, Brian is working on becoming a chemical engineer, so he can work in the space program someday.

Brian was born on September 11, 1977. His mom and dad are Patsy and Pat Roybal. He has a brother, Adam, and a sister, Tamara. The Roybal family is very active in the community. They go to Notre Dame Catholic Church and take part in lots of church activities. Brian plays basketball with his family and his cousins, who live next door. He also takes karate. When he earned a black belt, it had his name on it in Korean and in English.

In 1994, Brian and thousands of other kids went to World Youth Day in Denver, Colorado. People came from all over the world to take part and see Pope John Paul II. More than 300,000 people celebrated Mass with the Pope. Brian will never forget the excitement of young people from all around the world praying together and sharing their faith.

For more than ten years, Brian has been active in scouting programs. He started in Cub Scouts when he was seven. His dad was the leader of his pack and Brian loved doing things with him. As he grew older, Brian continued to work hard to become an Eagle Scout—the highest honor one can achieve in Scouting. To do this, he had to find a special project and get the approval of all his scout leaders. The theme of Brian's

project was, "The family that reads together, succeeds together." Brian made 30 book-cases and collected books to fill the shelves. He gave them to people who didn't have very much money. Brian even found books written in Spanish for some people.

When Brian became an Eagle Scout, he got a letter from President Clinton, the Navy, the Army, and Governor Roy Romer. All the letters congratulated him for working to achieve this honor.

Brian tries to make his community a better place for people. He helps children learn to appreciate and be proud of their Chicano heritage. Brian teaches others to believe in

their culture, set goals for themselves, and work hard to achieve them. We think these things make Brian Roybal a true Chicano hero for children today.

CHARLOTTE LOPEZ

When Charlotte Lopez was crowned Miss Teen U.S.A., she was so happy she almost cried. This was a wonderful time for her, but things had not always been easy.

Charlotte Lopez was born in Puerto Rico on September 15, 1976. When she was a year old, she moved to Vermont with her mother, brother Duane, and sister Diana. Her mother struggled to take care of them. It was very hard for young Charlotte. Finally, she and her sister were put in a foster home. Their brother was sent to a different foster home. Charlotte and her sister lived in six different foster homes over the years. They got to stay with one family for 11 years. In this family, she got to go to the same school and church for a long time. They also did ballet and had piano lessons. Charlotte really liked this family, but was sad because they couldn't adopt her. She wanted a permanent family.

Then something wonderful happened. A friendly couple had been planning to adopt a young child. When they met Charlotte, she was 16, but they liked her so much, they adopted her anyway. From that time on, Charlotte Lopez has had a real home and real parents. She was excited that she was finally adopted. Now she has a permanent place to stay. Someday when she has children, they will have real grandparents.

Charlotte Lopez

In November 1992, Charlotte was in a beauty pageant. She did such a good job that she was crowned Miss Vermont Teen U.S.A. In August of 1993, she went to Mississippi for the national contest. She wore a dress that cost only $38. She wanted to show that money didn't matter. She believed that what really counted was what was inside.

The judges must have agreed because Charlotte Lopez became the new Miss Teen U.S.A. She won a new car and trips to Disneyland and Hawaii. She also won $40,000 cash. She hopes her position as Miss Teen U.S.A. will allow her to help kids in foster care. Today, Charlotte is in college studying broadcasting. She is also working on a book about foster care she wants to call *Lost in the System*. Charlotte hopes her book will teach people that foster children are not delinquents. She wants people to understand that children are put in foster care because their parents are unable to take care of them, not because they are bad kids. There are more than 500,000 children in foster care in the United States, and Charlotte wants people to know that they are good kids.

Charlotte Lopez learned that she had to stand up for herself because her parents weren't there for her. Charlotte showed us that things don't always go the way you want, but if you try your hardest, you can make your dreams come true—and help other people, too!

OUR VISION FOR A BETTER TOMORROW

By reading this book, we hope you've learned,
We, as all people, make the world turn.
Everyone is different in their own special way,
We want you to know that this is OK.

We have enjoyed learning about the Hispanic heritage. It's hard to tell you about everything we learned and everything we would like others to know. One of the most important things we found out is that all people are special. Those of us who are Hispanic enjoyed celebrating our heritage. Those of us who aren't Hispanic learned a lot, and it made us want to learn more about our own heritages.

We believe the world would be a better place if we all knew more about our own family's heritage. When you learn about your culture, you become interested in the culture of others. This helps you reach out and learn even more. We challenge you to think about who you are and to study more about yourself. Then people can learn about you.

Each of us needs to help make our country stronger by showing respect to all Americans. We are many colors, speak many languages, practice many customs, and come from many places. We all bring special gifts to America. If we learn to appreciate the gifts that everyone brings, our country will be a better place.

STUDENT AUTHORS
(First Edition)

Adrianne Aleman
Dominic Atencio
James B. Barela
Nichole C. Bargas
Bryan Brammer
Kevin Brand
Kimberly Burnell
Rachel Caliga
Rocio M. Chavez
Nicole Cook
Anastasia Cordova
Christopher deBree
Olivia deBree
Karina deOliviera
Brandon Dudley
Jennifer Flores-Sternad
Asia Garcia
Jaya Garcia
Amanda Gomez
Lanette Gonzales
Sergio Gonzales
Vanessa Gonzales
Brittany Hanson
Jenna Maria Helms
Heather Herburger
Jared Daniel Herrera
Cambri Hilger
Maria Hodge

Troy D. Holder
Aimee Hull
Christopher Husted
Amy Jessop
Ryan Joyce
Justin Juarez
Roxana Juarez
Greg Karsten
Whitney Kastelic
Perry D. Kline
Michael Laydon
Ben Lowry
Aymber E. Mackenzie
Fernando Manrique
Gonzalo Manrique
Alisha Martinez
Erica J. Martinez
Melissa Medrano
Amber A. Montoya
Jacob Montoya
Daniel Murphy
Harrison Nealey
April Padilla
Christina Marie Padilla
Roberto Padilla
Clint A. Parker
Vickie Pepper
Josh Jesus Pettit
Emily Phelan
Brian Quinn
Victor Quinonez Jr.
Cliff M. Rodriguez
Danelle M. Rodriguez
Desiree M. Rodriguez
Sarah Lynn Romero
Lance Ruybal
Nick Sanchez
Matthew Sandoval
Valerie Karla Schultz
Jennifer Shouse
Ricky Stevens

Student authors

Margaret Stillman
Kimberly Sturk
Addie Jo Suazo
Donna Swigert
Laura Swigert
Anne Tatarsky
Kimberly Trujillo
Judy Beth Urteaga
Candace Elisa Valencia
Tommy C. Venard
Lara K. Vette
Angie Wegher
Brandon Weinberger
Jenny L. Wrzesinski

STUDENT AUTHORS
(Second Edition)

Josh Ackerman
Brian Annes
Steve Armijo
Yolanda Rios Azua
MaryBeth Bachmann
Carlo Bertolli
Damon Candelaria
Laura Chavez
Lindsay Christopher
Lynn Costanza
Stephan Csuk
Kent Dallow
Elizabeth Marie Daly

Student authors

Megan Davalos
Adam Dial
Leonel Noriega Diaz
Sergio Dominguez
Ronnie Felix
Ian Fidler
Blake Fiorito
Arleen Gonzalez
Erica Gonzalez
Eric Hanek
Emilie Nicole Hanson
Heydi Hau Chi
Jonathan Hoenig
Linda Irwin
Lalena Jaramillo
Andrea K. Johnsen
Roxana Juarez
Monica Kadnuck
Natalie A. Kruk
Brian Kura
Joelle Lacrue
Irene Lopez
Anastacio Mares
Danielle Mariscal
Jose Martinez III
Julio Martinez
Nathan Martinez
Shannon McCue
Natalie Medrano
Chrisandra Meindle
Manual Miramontes
Rebecca Monaghan
Natalie Moore
Jesus Munoz
Brian Noble
Eric Noble
Ian O'Bryon
Richard Padilla
Josh Pettit
Joey Pettit
Jim Pierce
Mike Psaltis
Domingo Puc
Jim Puls

Lindsay Ramirez
Joseph Ramos
Matthew Recsetar
Julia Rewerska
Stephanie Robotham
Jose Rodriguez
Sindia Rodriguez
Monica Ruybal
Natasha Ruybal
Dan Saavedra
Kelle Salzmann
Kimberly Sanchez
Corey James Shapiro
Jessica Stuckey
Christopher M. Suba
Sarah Swetlic
Tanya Tabic
Juan Valdez
Keith Wisniewski
Heather Zimny
Sherry Stumbaugh
Harvey Torrey
Andra Vette

TEACHER PARTICIPANTS
(First Edition)

Angelique Acevedo (Consultant)
Annette M. Acevedo-Martinez
Alex Gill Balles
Pia R. Borrego
Jean Tiran Cable
Judith H. Cozzens (Co-Director)
Mary Ann Garcia-Pettit
Lorraine Gutierrez
Helen Cozzens Healy (Co-Director)
Marsha Herald
Jan Lahlum
Jerry Lassos
Martin Laydon
Tria Lopez
Jean Makalusky-Martinez
José A. Martinez
Maria Ortiz-Venard

Melanie Shioya-Davis
Sherry Strumbaugh
Harvey Torrey
Andra Vette

TEACHER PARTICIPANTS
(Second Edition)

Donna Burris
Rebecca Compton
Mary Ann Corder
Pablo D. Espinoza
Robbin R. Kitashima
Stafie Parker

Lorena E. Poppleton
Sandra Quezada
Estelle Quinlan

OTHER PARTICIPANTS

Jeff Horan (editor)
Jari Kolterman (editor)
Martin Laydon (photographer)
Katherine S. Parker (photographer)
Kimberly Jo Peterson (editor)
Dorothy Poppleton (mentor)
Shelby W. Shrigley (editor)

Teacher participants

CALENDAR

Hispanic Americans celebrate many of the same holidays other Americans do, but they also might celebrate holidays, celebrations, and festivals from their native countries. This calendar is a list of some important dates for Hispanic Americans. Many of these holidays and special events fall on different days every year. Call ahead to confirm dates and times. Certain occasions, such as Cinco de Mayo and Hispanic Heritage Month, feature celebrations across the U.S.

January
Sonora Showcase, mid-January, (Arizona)—This fiesta in Yuma promotes the state of Sonora, Mexico. Features dancers, food and beverage samples, vacation information, and curios. For more information, contact the Yuma Civic and Convention Center, 1440 Desert Hills Drive, Yuma, AZ 85364; (602) 344-3800.

February
Charro Days, last Thursday of February, (Texas)—A colorful celebration of the Charro horseman of Mexico, a man of great riding skills. Dances, parades and a carnival. Contact Charro Days, Inc., P.O. Box 3247, Brownsville, TX 78523; (210) 542-4245.

Ybor City Fiesta Day, mid-February, (Florida)—A cultural celebration of many different ethnic groups. Contact Ybor City Chamber, 1800 East 9th Street, Tampa, FL 33605; (813) 248-3712.

March
Carnaval Miami, early-March, (Florida)—The biggest Hispanic festival in the United States, attracting nearly 1 million people for its final day. Ten days of concerts, parades, youth entertainment, sports events, ethnic foods, contests, and street dancers. For more information, contact Kiwanis Club of Little Havana, 1312 S.W. 27 Avenue, Third Floor, Miami, FL 33145; (305) 644-8888.

April
Fiesta San Antonio, mid- to late-April, (Texas)—A ten-day celebration including the week of April 21 (San Jacinto Day). Features parades, carnivals, sports, fireworks, music,

feasts, artwork, and dance. For more information, contact Fiesta San Antonio Commission, Inc., 122 Heiman Street, San Antonio, Texas 78205; (210) 227-5191.

Tucson Festival (Arizona)—An annual three-weekend celebration featuring fairs and special events promoting and preserving the cultural heritage of the Southwest and its regional arts and crafts. Includes the San Xavier Pageant Fiesta, a living-history reenactment with Spanish priests, conquistadors, mountain men, and the cavalry, as well as mariachi music, bonfires, fireworks, and traditional foods and dances. For more information, contact the Tucson Festival Society, Inc., 2720 East Broadway, Tucson, AZ 85716; (520) 622-6911.

Youth Mariachi Festival, spring–summer, (California)—Features young mariachis showcasing skills that have been passed down through generations. Contact La Casa de San Gabriel Community Center, 203 East Mission Drive, San Gabriel, CA 91776; (818) 286-2144.

May

Festival de Cinco de Mayo, May 5, (U.S. and Mexico)—A festival in honor of Mexican Independence Day. Celebrations include mariachis,

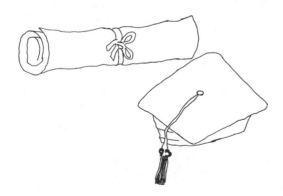

singers and dancers, arts and crafts shows, and ethnic foods. There may be a celebration near you. Here are a few locations and organizations to contact:

—Arizona: Phoenix Chamber of Commerce, 201 North Central, Suite 2700, Phoenix, AZ 85073; (602) 254-5521.

—California: Los Angeles Visitor's Bureau, 685 South Figueroa Street, Los Angeles, CA 90017; (213) 689-8822.

—Oregon: Portland-Guadalajara Sister City Association, P.O. Box 728, Portland, OR 97207; (503) 292-5752.

—Illinois: The Navy Pier, 600 East Grand Avenue, Chicago; (312) 595-7437

—Texas: The Market Square, 514 West Commerce Street, San Antonio TX 78207; (210) 207-8600.

Fiesta de Mayo (Arizona)—Annual celebration with sister city of Nogales across the Mexican border. Features mariachi bands, a bullfight in Mexican Nogales, dances, parades, and special Mexican foods. For more information, contact the Nogales Chamber of Commerce, Nogales, AZ 85621; (520) 287-3685.

Festival of Nations, early May, (Minnesota)— An enormous ethnic party the first week of the month. Nearly 100 different ethnic groups are represented, guest performers, food, folk art, cultural exhibits, and more. Contact the International Institute of Minnesota, 1694 Como Avenue, St. Paul, MN 55108; or call the Office of the Festival of Nations, (612) 647-0191.

Latin Music Festival, late May, (Illinois)—An annual event which includes music, entertainment, ethnic foods, and 400,000 visitors. Contact the Mayor's Office of Special Events Hotline at (312) 744-3316.

Fiesta de la Primavera (California)—A four-day celebration of spring which recreates California's historic Spanish era. Features an art show, historical exhibits, mariachis, and a buffalo barbeque. For more information, contact the San Diego Chamber of Commerce, 233 A Street, Suite 300, San Diego, CA 92101; (619) 232-0124.

June

El Paso Mariachi Festival (Texas)—Features mariachi bands, booths, and entertainment. Contact the Hispanic Chamber of Commerce; (915) 566-4066.

Mexican Town Mercado, late June through September, (Michigan)—An open-air festival and market with farmers, vendors, and different themes each week. Held every Sunday through September. For more information contact the Mexican Town Community Development Corporation, 7752 West Vernor Street, Detroit, MI 48209; (313) 842-0450.

New Mexico Arts and Crafts Fair, late-June, (New Mexico)—Annual fair at the New Mexico Fairgrounds. Contact the New Mexico Arts and Crafts Fair, 5500 San Mateo NE, Suite 105, Albuquerque, NM 87109; (505) 884-9043.

Spanish Night Watch, third weekend of June, (Florida)—Torch-light procession with 300 living-history actors in period dress. The public is invited to participate. Contact the Committee for the Nightwatch, 6315 County Road 208, St. Augustine, FL 32092; (904) 824-9550.

Youth Mariachi Festival, mid-June, (California)—An annual festival featuring the talents of young people in the art of mariachi. Contact La Casa de San Gabriel Community Center, 203 East Mission Drive, San Gabriel, CA 91776; (818) 286-2144.

July

Fiesta de Santiago y Santa Ana, late-July, (New Mexico)—This Taos celebration in honor of the saints includes a Mass and procession, music , entertainment, a children's parade, arts and crafts, and food. Contact the Fiesta Council at (505) 776-8269.

Hispanic American Cultural Festival, late-July, (Washington, D.C.)—Contact the Washington, D.C. Convention and Visitor's Association, 1212 New York Avenue, NW, Suite 600 Washington, D.C. 20005; (202) 835-1555.

San Luis Rey Fiesta and Barbecue, late-July, (California)—An annual two-day celebration which includes an Old World "Blessing of the Animals," food, arts and crafts, Mexican and Spanish dancers, musicians, actors, games, rides, street dancing, Mexican-style barbecue, and

an outdoor Mass. For more information, contact the San Diego Convention and Visitors Bureau, 1200 Third Avenue, Suite 824, San Diego, California 92101; (619) 232-3101, or write Brother Howard Casey, Old Missions, 133 Golden Gate, San Francisco, California 94102.

August

San Clemente Fiesta, mid-August, (California)—Live music, ethnic foods, and children's games. Contact the San Clemente Chamber of Commerce, 11000 North El Camino Real, San Clemente, CA 92672; (714) 492-1131.

Basque Festival (Oklahoma)—Contact the Boise City Chamber of Commerce; (405) 544-3344. Celebrates the culture of the Basque people, who live in the mountains between Spain and France.

Old Adobe Fiesta (California)—Craftspeople show visitors how to make candles, baskets, bread, and butter. Entertainment includes Hispanic bands, square dancers and contests. Con-

tact Old Adobe Association, P.O. Box 631, Petaluma, CA 94953; (707) 762-4871.

September

Carnival Latino (Louisiana)—Annual New Orleans festival includes a parade, food, and entertainment. For more information, call (504) 581-2001 or (504) 585-7262.

Heritage Week (Oklahoma)—Features ethnic festivities along with the annual Osage County Fair. Exhibits, a carnival, and entertainment. Contact the Osage County Farm Agent, (918) 287-4170.

National Hispanic Heritage Month, September 15–October 15, (Nationwide)—Many different celebrations and programs around the nation in honor of Hispanic heritage.

Hispanic Heritage Month Celebrations, mid-September–mid-October, (Minnesota)—Includes dance, arts, and music workshops, ethnic foods, Latin jazz and salsa dances, and more. For more information, contact the Instituto de Arte Y Cultura, 3501 Chicago Avenue South, Minneapolis, MN 55407; (612) 824-0708.

Santa Fe Fiesta, (New Mexico)—Annual Hispanic religious celebration with parties, parades, and religious ceremonies. Contact the Santa Fe Convention and Visitor's Bureau, P.O. Box 909, Santa Fe, NM 87504; (800) 777-2489.

Adams-Morgan Day (Washington, D.C.)—Features Hispanic festivities. Contact the Convention and Visitor's Association, 1212 New York Avenue, Suite 600, Washington, D.C. 20005; (202) 789-7000.

Mexican Independence Parade and Fiesta (California)—Parade, arts and crafts, music, and food in celebration of Mexican Independence Day. For more information, contact the Mexican Cultural Center at (916) 363-1610.

October

The Day of the Dead, late-October, (U.S. and Latin America)—A popular holiday for people to show respect for their dead relatives. Celebrations are held throughout the U.S.

Hispanic Heritage Festival, October 1–31, (Florida)—Commemorates the discovery of America by Christopher Columbus, and the Hispanic contribution to the economic and cultural development of Florida. For more information, contact the Hispanic Heritage Council, Inc., 4011 West Flagler Street, #505, Miami, FL 33134; (305) 541-5023.

International Heritage Fair, late-October, (California)—A two-day fair celebrating the heritage and contributions of the diverse ethnic

groups that make up the history and population of Los Angeles. For more information contact the L.A. Visitor's Bureau, 685 South Siguero Street, Los Angeles, CA 90017; (213) 689-8822.

November

La Posada de Kingsville (Texas)—Festivities for this Christmas tradition begin the weekend before Thanksgiving and continue through mid-December. Includes a Parade of Lights. Contact the Kingsville Convention and Visitor's Bureau, P.O. Box 1562, Kingsville, TX 78364; (800) 333-5032.

December

Las Posadas (U.S. and Latin America)—A Christmas story of Spanish heritage which tells how Joseph and Mary searched for a place for Christ to be born. Celebrations and plays are held in many communities around the U.S.

Feast of Our Lady of Guadalupe, December 12, (New Mexico)—In honor of the patron saint of Mexico. Contact the Santa Fe Convention and Visitor's Bureau, P.O. Box 909, Santa Fe, NM 87504; (800) 777-2489.

Fiestas Navidenas (Texas)—This Christmas festival is held annually in San Antonio. Includes piñata parties, blessing of the animals, and a visit from Poncho Claus. For more information, contact Market Square, 514 West Commerce Street, San Antonio, TX 78201; (210) 207-8600.

RESOURCE GUIDE

Here is a list of Hispanic-related organizations that might be of use to you. For more information, please see the Calendar on page 140.

Arizona

Movimiento Artistico Del Rio Salado, 1201 South 1st Avenue, Phoenix, AZ 85003; (602) 253-3541. Holds visual arts exhibitions and workshops with emphasis on Hispanic traditional and contemporary imagery, particularly in Mexican American culture. Open Tuesday to Friday, 11 a.m.–4 p.m.

California

Aztlan Cultural, 477 15th Street, Ste. 200, Oakland, CA 94612; (415) 834-7897. Promotes literary and visual expression throughout the Spanish speaking community of the Bay area. Features artistic, cultural, and educational programs.

Galeria de la Raza/Studio 24, 2857 24th Street, San Francisco, CA 94110; (415) 826-8009. Includes individual, group, and theme exhibits. Folk-art exhibits and sales. Open daily, 12 p.m.–6 p.m.

The Mexican Museum, Fort Mason Center, Building D, Laguna & Marina Blvd., San Francisco, CA 94123; (415) 441-0445. Reveals the ever-changing history of Mexican art and culture. Includes pre-Hispanic art, colonial art, folk art, Mexican fine art, and Mexican American fine art. Open Wednesday to Sunday, 12 p.m.–5 p.m. Admission is free to members and children under age 10; $3 for adults; $2 for seniors and students.

La Casa de San Gabriel Community Center, 203 East Mission Drive, San Gabriel, CA 91776; (818) 286-2144. Provides education, health care, and social services for the community, and sponsors several events throughout the year.

Colorado

Museo de las Americas, 861 Santa Fe Drive, Denver, CO; (303) 571-4401. Exhibits Hispanic art, culture, and history. Latin America and the American Southwest are featured, and exhibits change throughout the year. Open Tuesday to Saturday, 10 a.m.–5 p.m. Admission is free for kids; $3 for adults; $2 for seniors and students.

Connecticut

Puerto Rican/Latin American Cultural Center, University of Connecticut, 267 Glenbrook Road, U-188, Storrs, CT 06269; (203) 486-2204. Promotes Puerto Rican and Latin American culture through art, dance, and music.

Spanish Cultural Association, 160 Ferry Street, New Haven, CT 06513; (203) 787-0169. A community service group promoting cultural activities, including dance.

Florida

Ancient Spanish Monastery, St. Bernard de Clairvaux Cloisters, 16711 West Dixie Hwy., North Miami Beach, FL 33160; (305) 945-1462. Exhibits paintings and sculpture and sponsors art festivals and drama. Open daily, 10 a.m.– 4 p.m. Admission is $1 for kids age 12 and under; $4.50 for adults.

Cuban Museum of Arts and Culture, 1300 SW 12th Avenue, Coral Gables, FL 33129; (305) 858-8006. Gathers works of art, historic documents, and relics of Cuban heritage. Sponsors an educational outreach program. Hours by appointment.

The Spanish Quarter Museum, P.O. Box 1987, St. Augustine, FL 32085; (904) 825-6830. Collections include Spanish and Spanish-colonial artifacts. Maintains library and outdoor museum of 20 restored buildings of the eighteenth and nineteenth centuries. Open daily, 9 a.m.–5 p.m. Admission is $2.50 for kids ages 6–18; $5 for adults. Free for kids age 6 and under.

Georgia

Asociacion Cultural Hispanoamericano (ACHA), P.O. Box 1083, Augusta, GA 30903; (404) 733-7394. Promotes Latin American culture through art, dance, poetry, music, and geographical and historical programs.

Illinois

Casa Aztlan, 1831 South Racine Avenue, Chicago, IL 60608; (312) 666-5508. Bilingual and bicultural organization providing classes, theatrical productions, children's programs, and art exhibits.

Juan Antonio Puerto Rican, Cultural Center, 1671 North Claremont, Chicago, IL 60647; (312) 342-8023. Sponsors numerous cultural activities including mini-festivals, parades, folkloric dance groups, Puerto Rican and Latin American poetry readings, and mural paintings.

Latino Youth, 1827 West Cullerton, Chicago, IL 60608; (312) 829-0181. Group of high school students involved in the production, performance, publication, and exhibition of community art. Provides instruction in the visual, literary, and performing arts.

Mexican Fine Arts Center Museum, 1852 West 19th Street, Chicago, IL 60608; (312) 738-1503. Sponsors special events and exhibits Mexican and contemporary folk art. Open daily, 10 a.m.–5 p.m. Admission is free.

Michigan

Casa de Unidad, 1920 Scotten, Detroit, MI 48209; (313) 843-9598. Identifies, develops, and preserves Hispanic cultural heritage of southwest Detroit. Offers workshops in the arts, operates a bilingual print shop, and sponsors films, concerts, and an annual festival.

Our Lady of Guadalupe Mission, 3110 Goulden Street, Port Huron, MI 48060; (810) 985-5212. Sponsors three Hispanic celebrations annually. Offers classes, workshops, and other activities in folk culture and the visual and performing arts.

Minnesota

Instituto de Arte y Cultura, 3501 Chicago Avenue, Minneapolis, MN 55407; (612) 824-0708. Provides cultural and educational services to Hispanic and non-Hispanic communities through its performing arts series, storytelling, folkloric dance classes, music and mariachi concerts, and visual arts exhibits.

Missouri

Guadalupe Center, 2641 Belleview, Kansas City, MO 64108; (816) 561-6885. Promotes Hispanic culture by sponsoring community activities of different kinds.

New Mexico

Millicent Rogers Museum, PO Box A, Taos, NM 87571; (505) 758-2462. Contemporary exhibitions include religious and secular arts of Hispanic New Mexico. Open daily, 10 a.m.–5 p.m. Admission is $2 for kids; $4 for adults.

Museum of International Folk Art, 706 Camino Lejo, Santa Fe, NM; (505) 827-6350. Exhibits Spanish Colonial religious art, Southwest Hispanic folk art, and furniture. Open daily, 10 a.m.–5 p.m. Admission is free for kids age 16 and under; $4.20 for adults.

Spanish History Museum, 2221 Lead SE, Albuquerque, NM 87106; (505) 268-9981. Exhibits reveal the Hispanic role in U.S. history, such as Spanish assistance to George Washington's revolutionary army. Open daily, 1 p.m.–5 p.m. Free for kids age 12 and under; $1 for adults.

New York

Americas Society, 680 Park Avenue, New York, NY 10021; (212) 249-8950. Devoted to promoting Latin America culture, politics, and economics. Upcoming exhibits include: "Maria

Izquierdo: A Retrospective" (Spring, 1997); "The Colonial Art of Potosi" (Fall, 1997); "The Soul of Spain: Spanish Folk Art and Its Transformation in the Americas" (Fall, 1998). The society also organizes exhibitions which tour the country.

Casa Cultural Dominicano, 4050 Broadway, New York, NY 10032; (212) 740-2223. Sponsors art exhibits, concerts, dances, theatrical presentations, and literary events.

El Bohio/Charas Cultural Center, 605 East 9th Street, New York, NY 10009; (212) 533-6835. Sponsors Spanish folkloric dances, art exhibits, bilingual plays, and cabaret nights.

El Museo del Barrio, 1230 Fifth Avenue, New York, NY 10029; (212) 831-7272. Museum established to protect the cultural heritage of Latin Americans. Displays the work of contemporary Puerto Rican and Latin American visual artists, including diverse media and experimental works. Upcoming exhibits include "The Tainos Legacy of the Caribbean" (Summer, 1997). Open Wednesday to Sunday, 11 a.m.–5 p.m.; Thursday, 12 p.m.–7 p.m. Free for kids under age 12; $2 for students; $4 for adults.

El Puente, 211 South 4th Street, Brooklyn, NY 11211; (718) 387-0404. Offers extensive cultural opportunities for Hispanic groups and individuals, and sponsors workshops, exhibits, a drama club, and a dance ensemble.

Hispanic Society of America, Broadway at 155th Street, New York, NY 10039; (212) 690-0743. Seeks to preserve Spanish culture. Museum and library devoted to the arts and culture of the Iberian Peninsula from prehistoric

times to the present. Collections include literary works and artifacts. Open Tuesday to Saturday, 10 a.m.–4:30 p.m.; Sundays, 1 p.m.–4 p.m. Admission is free.

The New Museum of Contemporary Art, 583 Broadway, New York, NY 10012; (212) 219-1355. Collections include the work of new Latin American artists. Open from Wednesday to Sunday, 12 p.m.–6 p.m., Saturday, 12 p.m.–8 p.m. Admission is free.

Taller Latinoamericano, 63 East 2nd Street, New York, NY 10003; (212) 777-2250. Sponsors theatrical and musical productions, art exhibitions, dances, lectures and demonstrations, and video presentations.

Pennsylvania

Taller Puertorriqueño, Inc., 2721 North 5th Street, Philadelphia, PA 19133; (215) 426-3311. Preserves, develops, and promotes Puerto Rican artistic and cultural traditions, and supports a better understanding of other

Latin American cultures and our common heritage. Publishes a calendar of events.

Texas

El Paso Museum of Art, 1211 Montana Avenue, El Paso, TX 79902; (915) 541-4040. Focuses on Hispanic history and art. Open Tuesday, Wednesday, Friday, Saturday, 9 a.m.–5 p.m.; Thursdays, 9 a.m.–9 p.m.; Sundays, 1 p.m.–5 p.m. Admission is free.

Guadalupe Cultural Arts Center, 1300 Guadalupe Street, San Antonio, TX 78207; (210) 271-3151. A multi-disciplinary Hispanic arts and cultural institution offering instructional programming and presentations. Stages dance, music, and theatrical productions, and offers photography, painting, and drawing classes.

International Museum of Cultures, 7500 West Camp Wisdom Road, Dallas, TX 75236; (214) 709-2406. An ethnographic museum portraying indigenous, contemporary people living in remote areas of the world. Open Tuesday to Friday, 10 a.m.–5 p.m., Saturday to Sunday, 1:30 p.m.–5 p.m. Admission is free.

McAllen International Museum, 1900 Nolana, McAllen, TX 78504; (210) 682-1564. Exhibits Mexican folk art and offers educational programs which emphasize Hispanic contributions. Permanent exhibits include "Textiles of the Southwest." Open Tuesday to Saturday, 9 a.m.–5 p.m., Sunday, 1 p.m.–5 p.m. Fifty cents for kids 12 and under; $2 for adults.

Mexic-Arte Museum, 419 Congress Avenue, Austin, TX 78701; (512) 480-9373. Exhibits include the work of young Latino artists as well as art from the Augustín Casasola Archive. Also

includes photographs of the Mexican Revolution; El Taller de la Grafica Popular/The Workshop of Popular Graphics; and Masks from Guerrero. Open Monday to Saturday, 10 a.m.–6 p.m. Admission is free.

San Antonio Museum of Art, 200 West Jones Avenue, San Antonio, TX 78215; (210) 978-8100. Includes pre-Columbian, Spanish colonial, and Mexican folk art. Open daily, 10 a.m.–5 p.m.; Tuesday, 10 a.m.–9 p.m.; Sunday, 12 p.m.–5 p.m. Admission is $1.75 for kids; $4 for adults.

Washington, D.C.

Art Museum of the Americas, 201 18th Street NW, Washington, D.C. 20006; (202) 458-6016. One of the premier collections of Latin American art in the United States. Open from Tuesday to Saturday, 10 a.m.–5 p.m. Admission is free.

Centro de Arte, 1470 Irving Street NW, Washington, D.C. 20010; (202) 483-7755. Promotes artistic expression in Washington, D.C. through exhibits, children's workshops, dance performances, bilingual theater productions, and Hispanic music.

INDEX

A

Acevedo II, Homero E., 122-124
Adivinanzas (riddles), 55, 58
Alamo, 13, 20
Alire, Rick, 130–131
All Saints' Day, 28
Alvarez, Luis, 80
American Telephone and Telegraph Company (AT&T), 122
Amezcua, Consuelo Gonzalez, 44
Apodaca, Jerry, 76
Arawaks, 3, 6
Archuleta, Diego, 20
Art, Hispanic, 43–53
Art projects, 49–54
Atencio, Sidney, 109–111
Aztecs, 1, 3–4, 7–8

B

Baez, Joan, 89–90
Barela, Casimiro, 21
Battle of Puebla, 27
Battle of San Jacinto, 13
Bilingual Education Act, 15
Bubonic plague, 10

C

Cabeza de Vaca, Alvarar Nuñez, 8–9
Canseco, Jose, 76
Carbajal, Michael, 101
Carr, Vicki, 88
Castro, Raul, 76
Cavazos, Lauro, 76
Central America, 3, 4
Chavez, Cesar, 15–17
Chavez, Dennis, 79
Chavez, Eduardo, 45
Chicano, 6
Chicken enchiladas, 4
Chistes (jokes), 55, 57–58
Chorizo con huevos, 34
Christmas plays (*Las Posadas*), 23–24
Christmas traditions, 23–25

Cinco de Mayo, 27
Cisneros, Evelyn, 97–98
Clemente, Roberto, 86–87
Cognates, 59
Colors (*Los colores*), 55, 60
Columbus, Christopher (Cristóbal Colón), 1, 4–6, 7
Cooking, 32–37
Congressional Medal of Honor, 75
Cortés, Hernán, 7–8
Coronado, Francisco de, 9
Costumes, for dance, 39
Crusade for Justice, 21
Cuba, 1, 2, 3, 6, 7, 17
Cuentos (stories), 62–74

D

Dances, 37–42
Dance Groups, 41
Day of the Dead, 27–28
Day of the Three Kings, 24–25
de Las Casas, Father, 7, 49
Dia de Los Muertos (Day of the Dead), 27–28
Dichos (sayings), 55
Diego, Juan, 63–65
Dominguez, Aianasio, 12
Drinks, 35–36

E

Easter eggs, 26
Easter season, 25–26
"El Grillo" ("The Cricket"), 66–69
"El Movimiento" (the Chicano movement), 44
El Museo del Barrio, 45, 46
"El Principe y Los Pájaros" ("The Prince and the Birds"), 70–71
Epiphany, 25
Escalante, Jaime, 84–85
Escalante, Silvestre Velez de, 12
Estefan, Gloria, 96–97
Explorers, 1, 4–10; Cabeza de

Vaca, 8–9; Columbus, 1, 4–6, 7; Cortés, 7–8; Ponce de Leon, 6–7

F

Feliciano, Jose, 92–93
Ferdinand, King, 4, 6
Fernandez, Giselle, 101
Fernandez-Mott, Alicia, 114–116
Festivals, 23–28; Cinco de Mayo, 27; Day of the Dead, 27–28; Day of the Three Kings, 24–25; Easter, 25–26; Epiphany, 25; Las Posadas, 23–24; Quinceanera, 29–31
Filigree art, 44
Flores, Carlos, M.D., 125–126
Flores, Patrick, 83–84
Flores, Tom, 76
Florida, 7, 17
Folk art, 43, 48–54
Foods, Spanish, 32–36
Fountain of Youth, 7
Frases (phrases), 55, 61
Fruit popsicles (*paletas*), 36
Fruit punch, 36

G

Garcia, Hector, 80–81
Garza, Carmen Lomas, 44–45
Golden Cross Award, 20
Gonzales, Bishop Roberto, 121–122
Gonzalez, Henry B., 103
Gonzales, Rudolfo ("Corky"), 21–22
Guacamole, 34
Guiteras, Juan, 78

H

Haciendas, 10
Halloween, 28
Hernandez, Ismael, 128–129
Hidalgo, Miguel, 12
Hispanic artists, 44–46; Amezcua,